# THE

# HOLLOW

## KAT HOSIER

QUILL HAWK PUBLISHING

The Hollow

Published by arrangement with Quill Hawk Publishing and Kat Hosier
Cover designed by Canva

Manufactured in the United States
ISBN 978-1-965142-74-5 (paperback)
ISBN 978-1-965142-75-2 (hardback)

Quill Hawk Publishing (Edmond, Oklahoma)

*If you love animals, I suggest you do not read this.*

*If you have religious beliefs, I suggest you do not read this.*

*If you want to be entertained, I suggest you turn the page.*

*-Kat*

# Part I: The Task

# Chapter 1

Two discs are launched from midair. Each disk plummets into an earthy pond about an acre in diameter. The pond reeks of sewage and fermentation, a smell that is clearly decades old. Each disk is approximately seven inches in diameter and begins to dissolve into the water as soon as it reaches its starting point. Inside the disk is a round silver coin that symbolizes a much larger exposition. Unlike the pond, this coin is hundreds of years old.

The moment the disks land in the center of the pond, a man and a woman simultaneously leap into the water. As they strive to beat the dissolving disk to the bottom of the coagulated water, they each vomit the last meal they most recently consumed. The rotting smell of bloated death infiltrates their nostrils, ultimately reaching their stomachs and unearthing every possible reflex. Floating atop the pond are various dead frogs, fish, and other remains that are no longer identifiable.

They hunker into the water and begin the unbearable journey downward. After sixty seconds, the man appears through the muck, his red curls covered in algae. He gasps for air and races toward the edge of the water. The woman cannot be located anywhere.

As he reaches the finishing line, an evil spirit comes from overhead and states, "You have conducted the first of three tasks. Your reward is as follows.

A bright glare appears in the eyes of the man. The woman appears on the edge of the water, her silver coin in hand. She is too late. The bright glare penetrates her heart, shooting a bolt of fire through her. Blood gushes from her every orifice, and she falls forward to her death. Her body evaporates into the unknown, as the man screams out in unbearable horror.

A home appears before the man—a beautiful, established two-story home with oak trees that gently cover a circular driveway. The house is inviting. The man, in shock, stumbles to the front door, crying out as he leaves a trail of stench and turns the knob. As he enters the home, he falls to his knees and sobs. Only an hour prior had he opened the letter, sealing his fate at fifty percent.

Frozen in terror and disbelief, the man clutches the cold, damp ground, the echoes of the woman's screams still ringing in his ears. For a long moment, nothing moves—the pond's surface returns to its unnatural stillness, the heavy odor hanging in the air as a grim reminder of what has just transpired. The man forces his trembling body to crawl from the water's edge, the weight of his victory pressing down like a stone on his chest.

The letter was on the entryway table in front of him. Angrily, he tears it up and slams it into the rug beneath him. From this moment on, his life will never be the same. He gathers his strength and makes his way to his feet. Channeling every ounce of courage he has left, he ventures through the home.

The home is eerily quiet, not like a normal home. He peers into the kitchen, laying eyes on a vintage-style refrigerator. Opening the door, he notices everything is dark inside. There is no power, no surge of electricity running through the walls, emitting the sound of a confirmed home. Picture frames line the halls and tables. An overwhelming sense of displacement washes over him like vertigo, as the man stares in disbelief at the frames. Every one of them is vacant. Not a single picture, not even the original display with the selling bar code, is present. Fear creeps over as he makes his way up the stairs. Creaking boards sound throughout the home as he unsteadily grasps the railing.

Turning right to a nearby bedroom, he makes his way into the unnaturally tidy space. He presses the drape in a swiping gesture, only to peer out to a desolate concrete wall right outside of the glass.

Rage forms, and the man shouts his first words. "Is this the end of time? Is this the afterlife? Where are my family members? Where is any form of LIFE? Why is this happening to me?"

As he falls to his knees, he hears a paper fall from midair. His words seem to vanish into emptiness, but the silence that follows is deafening. The chill in the air presses against his skin as if the house itself is holding its breath, waiting. The only reply is the echo of his own voice, ricocheting off the barren walls and lost among the shadows. He suddenly senses, with unnerving clarity, that he's being watched—a cold realization that something unseen lurks just beyond the edge of the light.

It is another letter. Gasping, he rages again, shouting profanities and begging for salvation of any kind. He kneels in a fetal position, praying for forgiveness. The sins of his nearby past have captured his full attention as he opens his eyes to the space underneath the perfectly made bed.

Approximately three feet in front of him lies a familiar object. Something or someone missed this valuable piece of ownership. The man reaches forward and grasps a worn, brown wallet. He opens the folds of the leather as an ounce of hope rekindles. Inside, there are cards, including an old Social Security card—Fredrick Ryan Robinson. As he places the card back into its sleeve, he turns an insert over to reveal a single photo. Falling back into the wall behind him, the man stares back at a familiar face. It is him. Next to him is a beautiful young woman with golden brown curls and stunning green eyes. Slight freckles dot her high cheekbones, and she appears to be in the prime of her twenties.

As Ryan pulls the picture out from the clear sleeve, he once more feels his reflexes regurgitate a green bile. Covered in drying alga, and now, in stomach bile, he cups his face in his hands and says a single word. "Renee." It has been his wife for almost two years. Ryan makes his way down the creaking stairs with letter, wallet, and photo in hand. Standing in front of the door, he opens the letter. A solitary line appears, written in an intimidating font.

**August 30th 2:45 p.m.**

It is the second task… for this afternoon.

He drops the letter and looks to his left at the old-fashioned clock on the wall. It reads 1:16 pm. His anxiety veers through his veins. Whatever awaits him is unknown. He turns the brass doorknob and opens the door to a new concrete wall. The oak trees disappear, and the pond is outdated. Staring blankly at the porous concrete, Ryan only has one thought left in his mind. Without hesitation, he simply says, "I am doing this for you, Renee."

He closes the door and sits down to conserve what little bit of strength he must prepare himself for the next challenge. Motivation floods as he closes his eyes and envisions Renee... and the fiery joust of fate that had sealed her death only moments before.

# Chapter 2

**August 12th**

"Mr. Robinson, will you please come to the main office?" The intercom overhead sounds throughout the entire grounds of Gregory Hall, the town's most upstanding Catholic high school. Renowned throughout the state of Texas, the school provides students with continuing education abroad in Rome or elsewhere of their choice, almost at once being accepted into the most prestigious programs due to the school's status. To teach here, a person must demonstrate unquestionable integrity, faith, and leadership.

As Ryan makes his way through the sea of green and gold regalia, he rounds the corner of the assistant's oversized oak desk, decked out in ridiculous monkey and gorilla ceramic decor—an overwhelming obsession of Ms. Wilson, a longtime faculty member.

The private office of Dr. Andrew Concord, an elderly principal of GH, is adjacent with a view overlooking the decadent lawn and garden out front. Entering the office, Ryan is greeted with a cascade of regret. Four heavy-set, clean-cut officers fill up the small, yet quaint Catholic office, leaving just enough room for the guest of honor.

"Good afternoon, Mr. Robinson. Have a seat," one of the officers says. "We have something we'd like to share with you, if you don't mind."

Without waiting for a response, the officer closest to the desk, tall and burly, with a stance anyone would fear, rudely turns a laptop around to face Ryan and presses play, almost gouging the "enter" button. Heavy breathing is expelled throughout the room as someone lets out a loud gulp. There on the small screen is a clear view of a man in a green suit and gold tie, with red curls and a gold Rolex watch, checking out at a local grocery store. The tall man pays with cash. Ryan feels his stomach drop to the bottom of his chair. The small audience continues to watch the laptop as the young sacker on the screen places the single purchase in the paper bag. The air in the room grows more intense as everyone stares in the same direction, their eyes glaring at the curly red-haired staff member who matches the description on the camera clip.

"Is this you?" An officer breaks the silence. "And can we verify that this has been a consistent purchase for you over the last three months?"

Ryan nods once as he looks up at the police officer.

The officer hands over multiple receipts for various transactions, each one paid with cash.  Each transaction aligns with the exact times shown on the cameras. "This item is not a common purchase for someone in this community, and it sent red flags to security guards in the store working on the camera footage," the officer says.

Without hesitation, Ryan admits to everything and is placed in cuffs. He is terminated at once from his position.

His upstanding title of "Teacher of the Year" for the entire nation is revoked twenty-four hours later, as news reports spread throughout the country.

***

Renee, alone at Ryan's and her home, has received multiple harassment calls, all from angry citizens, victims, and persistent reporters. She retreats into herself and quickly falls into a depression, struggling to cope with reality.

On bail, Ryan unacceptably arrives home. His sympathetic mother drops him off. Coming through the back door, Ryan finds Renee standing in the kitchen, her overall expression clearly doused in stress as she vigorously thumbed through a small notepad on the counter. Her face taut, she stared at the empty counter space, not realizing the beating the notepad was taking. Her mind seemed overtaken by the situation and what was to come.

The relentless glare of the television and the unwanted spotlight have turned every corner of their house into a prison. Each ring of the phone sends another wave of panic through Renee, and the constant barrage of notifications makes it impossible to find comfort. Ryan, now sitting across from her, senses her unraveling and feels powerless to help, his own shame and confusion pressing down on him like a physical weight. The silence between them grows heavier with each passing minute, as if both are waiting for something that might offer a reprieve from the chaos.

After about an hour of what seems like hell, a letter falls from the air. The troubled couple, in dismay, makes eye contact. Renee reaches over the hardwood floor that lines the kitchen and puts the letter on the island in front of her.

Renee hesitates, her hands trembling as she turns the envelope over, searching for any indication of its sender. The couple sits in shared dread, knowing that whatever waits inside could change their lives again. The clock ticks loudly in the background, marking each second, as Ryan leans forward, his voice barely above a whisper, "We must face this, Renee. Whatever it is, we can't ignore it." Her eyes fill with tears, but she nods, determined to confront the unknown together. For a moment, neither of them moves, the letter a silent threat between their trembling hands. The weight of the day seems to press down harder as they both stare at the unfamiliar handwriting, its presence amplifying the tension that already fills the air. With hesitant fingers,

Renee breaks the seal, her breath shaky, while Ryan braces himself for whatever cruel demand might be inside.

There, before their eyes, is simply a date and a time.

**August 30th 11:30 a.m.**

It is the first task, and it is in one hour.

# Chapter 3

Thirty seconds.

Fifteen seconds.

Five, four, three, two… Darkness falls over the entire home at 1123 Maple St., enveloping the home in pitch-blackness. An immediate sense of impending doom sweeps over Ryan's body. Realization sets in as he begins to understand what is happening. His chest is heavy, and his breathing slows due to a lack of space for his chest to inflate. Ryan is suffocating. This is the second task.

The fight is on. A substantial amount of dirt compresses his weakened body, as he struggles under the dense, earthy blanket. Gaining every possible centimeter of extra space, Ryan begins to leverage himself from the damp compression. He has been buried alive. Moist soil cakes his nostrils and eyelids, as his arms are pinned to his sides. He thrusts his hips one way, as his shoulders turn the opposite way. He realizes the reason behind this task. Ryan's worst fear is delivered by someone or something that knows of his past.

Ryan rapidly processes his thoughts. "Four minutes is often the amount of time a human has left before their brain cannot withstand any more loss of oxygen. Only four minutes. I must get out!"

For what seems like an eternity, Ryan thrashes himself to and from, loosening the mountain pressing against him. Now was not the time to wonder how he moved here within a split second. With no memory of the sudden transfer, he tosses what little bit he can of himself directly into a sharp object, puncturing the side of his right hand. Grabbing hold of the object, he uses its solidity to maneuver more soil surrounding his body.

After what seems like an eternity of fighting, a single hand forces itself through the summit of the mound, the sharp object in tow. The sensation of fresh, crisp air relieves the soiled hand, as his body moves more dirt, violently tormenting everything in its radius. His head surfaces in the fresh air, and he coughs and snorts out a dark drainage from his nostrils. His eyes burn with what resembles coffee grounds. Grit and grime fill his ears. Ryan is alive. His chest heaves in and out as a newborn would be fresh from a mother's womb.

"Fuck you!!" he shouts in rage. "What else do you have?" Rolling in the clean grass as a gesture to clean his body, he suddenly feels like a small animal, as they generally do the same to clean their bodies or satisfy an itch. "Fuck, I need FOOD." A dreadful desire for thirst consumes him.

Ryan leaps to his feet and notices he is in the middle of a familiar place. It is a giant open field, filled with tall grass around the borders—tall enough that an outsider could not see into the center of the location. It is the ideal place to hide, or to hide *something*. He peers down to realize he is completely naked. Yet, he knows exactly where he is and makes his way east through the tall grass and into the dense forest.

Nightfall is upon him as he continues in quest for fuel for his body. Barely able to make note of rocks and sticks, he feels each penetrating his bare feet as light becomes obsolete. It is now dark, and fear begins to well up inside. Finally, in the cool air of the night, underneath a sparsely lit sky, an old cabin takes shape through the trees and brushes. The cabin, over one hundred years old, has been vacant for over twenty years. The lead paint has chipped almost completely off the boards, and the windows' glass panes are caked with years of weathered dirt and appear milky to the naked eye. He makes his way up the few steps and lets out a cry as a piece of rotting wood jets into his left foot, making his cut to his inner thumb seem minuscule.

Reaching to turn the rusted knob of the dilapidated cabin, he remembers he never let go of the sharp, unidentified object. Once inside, a sudden flood of memories overtakes him, like that of a security blanket. It is his childhood getaway spot. It is the home of his grandparents, who are now in a long-term care facility upstate. He rarely goes to visit, as they are at the onset of dementia, and honestly doesn't make them a priority in his life.

As soon as the flood of childhood memories comes, how quickly they have gone. In an instant, all the positive times are replaced with atrocity and horror.

Evil lives on this property.

Ryan reaches into an old cupboard to pull out a dusty candle and an old box of matches; the entire door almost falls away from its squeaking hinges. After several strikes, the small candle illuminates the entire kitchen. Suddenly, a giant black rat darts across the counter, sending Ryan into a loud shrill, almost causing him to fall completely backward. It is then that he drops the sharp object onto the floor and finally acknowledges what he had been clinging to. Gazing over the six-inch object, he names it at once. It is the bone of a midsize animal. He reaches down to pick up the thigh bone and sets it on the dirty Formica counter.

His eyes lay intensely over the bone, studying it with precise knowledge, and then back to the cupboard. A single can of green beans is all that is available. With a violent motion, he retrieves a red brick from the front deck and slams the brick against the can, causing it to burst open on one side. The contents of over ten years' worth of expired food gush out to the floor and are easily compared to a dinner at The Ritz in the eyes of a man who hasn't eaten in what seems like an eternity. Ryan devours the beans as if he were a neanderthal, and with that, they were gone in a matter of seconds. A small wet patch on the tattered floor is all that remains. Ryan feels a hot gush of soupy liquid suddenly stream down his legs, so he dashes outside, diarrhea leaving an unvarying trail. The stench almost makes him vomit the beans.

Instincts lead him straight to a nearby outdoor well on the property. As he pumps the handle, he feels a fire underneath his hands, causing a fresh set of blisters. He realizes how badly he needs this and rinses his entire body with the ice-cold well water. It feels like heaven. Finishing, he looks up into the same familiar night sky that made his childhood so full. It reminds him that there is a bigger world, full of opportunity, and reassures him of a hopeful, brighter future. The stars and constellations remind him of a young boy who lived a detrimental life. The boy was him. He wanted to hide his demons and perfect his life, however he could. Looking down, he takes a deep breath.

From the woods nearby, and under the moonlight sky, the sound of footsteps rhythmically makes its way toward him. "Not a single human can be found in this part of Texas for miles. So, what the fuck could that be? Not a coyote," Ryan ponders.

He is in the middle of nowhere. His family still owns the property, but for undisclosed reasons decide to never to return to it. It remained untouched until now.

Terror paralyzes Ryan as he stands next to the well, barely able to gather the courage to run. Hearing clumps of heavy footsteps come closer, he takes off in a sprint towards the cabin.

His naked body feels the sensation of pricking needles as every nerve ending lights up in a state of shock. Ryan's wet body pierces through the night air. Bolting through the old wooden door, he backs away and stares at the door. Turning his head, he realizes the candle he had lit in the kitchen had burned down to the metal tray. It is almost pitch black in the home, except for the half-moon in the Texas night sky, casting out a selfish small amount of moonlight in the air.

Footsteps approach the cabin. The crunching sound of sticks and years of pine needles on the earth floor carries through the crisp night air. He follows the steps with his ears as they make their way onto the wooden deck, knowing by the weight and clacking sound of the feet that this is not a human. The clacking sounds like a donkey or goat's hooves striking a solid surface. The shadow of an unnaturally large, unknown figure shows through the cabin's cloudy glass panes against the Texas moon.

Panic sets in as Ryan hears a subtle turning of the rusted knob to the front door. With that, he quickly races down the small hall and hastily opens a narrow door in the center of the wall. Astonished and grateful, his grandparents left the old Mag light from the eighties. It still works. Turning the handheld light to his feet, he slowly raises it to show a full flight of steep, wooden stairs. Ryan clutches the tarnished railing for fear of plummeting to the floor below. Instantly, a small letter appears at the bottom of the stairs out of nowhere. Under his breath and in a state of pure horror, Ryan replies, "Oh my God…" His bare feet make contact with each step down into the basement, where they finally come within an inch of the letter. Trembling with fear, he kneels over and picks it up. The front door suddenly breaks open and makes a deafening strike against the interior wall of the entryway. Shaking the entire cabin, years of settled dirt fall from the overhead floorboards on top of Ryan's head and onto the letter.

The creature is in the house.

Ryan realizes he hasn't closed the door to the top of the stairwell. In a desperate attempt to find somewhere to hide, Ryan ducks to the back east corner of the basement, where the light is, and hastily tears open the letter. Petrified, his eyes well up with tears as his emotions overtake him. Staring down at the white paper, it simply reads:

**NOW**.

# Chapter 4

**August 12th**

Footsteps trot down the stairs of 1123 Maple St. A jovial Renee pours herself a cup of the English tea that had been steeping in a pot on the stove. A bouquet of freshly cut flowers from the front garden lights up the dining room as the morning sun greets every inch of the home. Outside, the birds chirp, and it seems like a perfect morning. A soft buzzing sound comes from a nearby end table beside a floral couch and Renee leans over to retrieve her cell phone. Looking down, she opens the short text from Ryan.

*"I will be a little late again today. I need to grade papers and set up for tomorrow's exam."*

"The beginning of the new school year is always stressful," Renee says aloud to herself. She ponders over the past months and feels an uneasy feeling come over her. Something isn't right, and her mind wanders. She makes her way into the garage knowing that Ryan has been spending more time there than usual. She searches through the organized bins and tools, only to find nothing. Driven by curiosity, Renee searches for any clue explaining Ryan's frequent daily absences. She does not trust him.

Turning her head to think, she looks down at the concrete and then up to the small window looking out back to the small lawn shed. There. She comes upon the double doors only to find that they are locked with a heavy-duty padlock. Ryan always has a company do their maintenance. Thinking aloud, Renee states to herself, "So, why the need for a lock?" Irritation and further curiosity peak her senses. Renee goes through the entire garage, kitchen, and office looking for a key. She finds nothing.

She decides to make the trip to the local hardware store and buys a strong set of bolt cutters. Returning home after the short trip, she throws her keys and wallet onto the counter and notices the time: 8:45 AM. She returns to the double doors of the small shed and forcefully clamps down on the metal lock. The cutters slide right off as she feels a small muscle pulling in her wrist. Growing even more angry, she retrieves the cutters and applies them directly on the same groove that she had left just on the lock. She presses the two long handles together as hard as she can and instinctively rotates them in a side-to-side motion, making the groove in the metal deeper. Suddenly, the padlock gives way, and the metal pieces separate. Renee drops the cutters in a sigh of relief and catches her breath. Removing the lock from the latch, she pushes the latch over and opens the two doors.

Gazing over the small space, approximately eight feet by ten feet, she notices how clean and unnecessary this shed is for their tidy property. "What a waste of space. I could literally use this as a she-shed," she thought. Not a single cobweb dawns the space. Only a couple of brown boxes are present, along with a few small tools on a shelf to the right. A perfectly coiled garden hose lies in the far-right corner. Stepping inside, breathing in the heavy, stale air, she notices a small basin just on the other side of the brown box furthest in the shed. Leaning over to examine beyond the basin, Renee discovers a large, yellow barrel with a locking lid. Taking a step back to evaluate the scene, she decides to open each box, one by one. The first box closest to the doors hold pool supplies, but they don't have a pool. When the couple want to swim, they go down to the neighborhood pool since they are part of an HOA.

Catching Renee's eyes at the bottom of the box are tiny green granules sparsely scattered throughout. What starts as a puzzled look on Renee's face, soon gives way to a startling revelation. Assessing the contents before her once more, Renee draws in a painful breath and looks down with acceptance. Heading back into the home, Renee phones the local police.

# Chapter 5

The police station is in the center of town. Easy accessibility is necessary to the community, so decades earlier the town voted to move the station to a historic downtown location, bringing back a sense of nostalgia and reviving the rundown street. Sitting at a square table in an interview room, Ryan takes every photograph with a flat effect as they are presented before him during the interrogation. The final photograph seals his fate as he realizes the local police have finally captured their community's pet predator.

A separate team resumes the delicate investigation at home. While in the shed, a team member pulls a loose floorboard from under the first box. The wood planks continue to lift, providing a precisely measured frame that conceals a large object. Lifting each of the wood planks, the team lay eyes on fresh dirt. Taking the flashlight, the officer lowers his head under the shed, scoping the area until he finds a large, flat tote that had been pushed back approximately three feet under the wood floor. The officer raises his head and announces what he sees as he begins to cough and gag. The stench is almost too much to bear.

Standing in the kitchen, Renee watches the scene unfold through the kitchen window.

Through the large, square opening in the floor, forensics pry opens the lid of the tote to reveal a large set of bones alongside various animal furs resembling those of cats, dogs, raccoons, and a red fox. A perfectly organized stack presents itself with extraordinary pride. A foul smell that had clearly deteriorated over time, continues to fill the air, turning stomachs throughout the small space. In a perfectly peaceful town, officers do not often discover this level of disturbance. The perimeter of the shed is closed off, and the tote is placed in the back of the squad van. Within the box next to the pool supplies are several smaller boxes containing small opaque bags filled with animal treats. Glancing at each treat, the officers notice tiny traces of green granules.

Each skin is studied and placed in an individual container at the station. The families who reported their pets missing are brought in individually to identify their beloved pets. Numerous animals are found; almost half the census is believed to be strays or wild animals of the nearby woods.

Renee hides from her in-laws, who plague her to the media as the main suspect of the murders. The horrid realization sets in, and she becomes angry as she reaches into an untouched cabinet of gin and wine. Days pass by, and she falls into a drunken, depressed state. Not eating anything without it coming back up, Renee refuses all contact with family and friends. Her employer gives her a temporary leave of absence. Extraordinarily little energy is left within her and with that, her strength weakens as she tours through the stages of grief alone. In the days that follow, Ryan's mother, Grace, gives a statement to the public in a pitiful attempt to redeem her son.

"My son is a highly respectable man in this state and the surrounding states. So, to be accused of something so outlandish is absurd! Why don't y'all look at his wife! Who called him in? Who opened the doors to the shed so forcefully to make it look like she never had a key, herself? I genuinely believe that she is the one to investigate since my son is so hardworking. Ryan deserves to be dismissed for this heinous crime. You people should be ashamed of yourselves. Stop grabbing at straws and turn your attention to the one who is claiming to be innocent!"

Several people in the crowd cheer, and others scream profanities at the woman. Bail is posted at a feasible amount as the investigation unfolds. Grace, alongside her husband, places the bond without hesitation and hires the most prestigious attorney in the area. Over time, the media draws back and allows Renee peace as a no trespassing sign is placed at her property line. The neighborhood, as angry as they are, buckle down on their own peace, realizing as an HOA, they want to maintain their status.

It is only a matter of days before Renee allows him back into their home to divide their property and begin their divorce proceedings before a potential trial. Over the course of the evening, Renee communicates to Ryan that she is ready to start a new life out of state, where she can focus on a better future and be welcomed into a new community where no one knows of her prior marriage and life. Showing a courageous amount of grace and patience, she focuses on settling her ties with Ryan, not knowing she is about to face the first task, leading to her premature death.

# Chapter 6

Trembling, Ryan quickly surveys the murky basement for possible items that can be used as a weapon. The basement, which holds little, leaves him with limited options. His right hand clutches the light so tightly it begins to cramp, sending aching pain through his palm and down into his fingers. Desperately, he retrieves a rusty pitchfork leaning against a nearby wall. The pitchfork has clearly been left out in the elements over the years, as a weathered handle begins to shoot splinters into Ryan's other hand. An enormous weight makes its way down the stairwell. With every clanking step against the wood, a nerve inside of Ryan's body ignites into a fiery penalization as the daunting presence of death overtakes the blackened room.

*"Clip, clop, clip, clop, CLIPPP, CLOPPP!"* Heavy hooves sludge down the steps as a flood of dread envelops Ryan's spirit. With

every step, the wood cracks as it unwillingly accepts the weight of something beyond its threshold.

Suddenly, the deathly shadow of a vast creature appears in the center of the room. Hardly illuminating its full frame through the upheaving dust bloom in the air, Ryan drops the light, his heart accelerating with adrenaline. The blackened, shadowy figure, too large to be human, struggles to fit within the basement parameters. Ryan viciously jolts side to side with an unsteady shaking of adrenaline-based fear. Slowly raising the light to regain his view, Ryan shines it upon the figure standing before him. Instinctively, he crawls backwards using his fists and feet, until the cold rock wall of the basement stops him from going further. Still completely naked, Ryan's body shudders as the wall sends shivers throughout his spine. Moist dirt packs his butt as he continues to nervously wedge himself back and forth. The tips of his ears burn from the freezing temperatures as snot drips incessantly from his nose. Tears flow once again from his eyes as emotions flood his mind.

Steadying his hands on the dirt floor below him, Ryan lets out a scream of panic as a black tarantula the size of a softball passes effortlessly over his right leg and crosses right over the shaft of his penis, which shrivels up inside his inner torso.

Looking at the demonic creature before him, Ryan feels a hot saturation pour between his inner thighs and downwards to his butt, creating a small pool beneath him. Steam rises against the winter air as a sour, pungent stench infiltrates the creature's senses, making it salivate all over its body.

The face hides in a shadowy cloak of fur. Bones protrude prominently beneath mismatched skins, as if a human had created an outfit from multiple animals. The visible patchworks of skins, bones, and furs are all Ryan focuses on. Accepting the limited options, Ryan looks up to the beast. Memories flood as he gazes in awe. The skeletal giant approaches, takes hold of Ryan's face, and cups it to show a tender love for the young man. Ryan's heart begins to relax, and his respirations slow to an unlabored pace. The sensation of compassion swells into a protective realm, a feeling that Ryan hasn't experienced since he was a small boy before his father became an alcoholic.

Gazing more closely, Ryan notices small, handwritten words on aged paper that have molded into the bones. They are words that he recognizes. Tears well up in Ryan's eyes as his defensive wall shatters with pure vulnerability. It is the first time in his life that Ryan feels true love. Taking in a slow and relieving breath, he lets it out as he subtly smiles.

For a fleeting moment, the world seems suspended in silence, the only sound Ryan can register is the deafening thud of his own heartbeat echoing in his ears. The creature's touch, unexpectedly gentle yet fraught with an ancient sorrow, lingers on his cheek, as if conveying a final, unspoken farewell. In that instant, Ryan senses a profound connection to something timeless and unknown, a force that both terrifies and soothes him. Jagged fingers of pure bone dive straight into Ryan's eye sockets, blood gushing down onto the floor. Retrieving his claws, the creature flaunts a set of spherical rings on his fingers- Ryan's eyeballs.

Yellow saliva drips all over the front of its body, and the creature takes its lengthy, slender fingers into its mouth, and sucks off each eye from its fingers, chewing them as they burst into its mouth, squirting blood all over Ryan's face.

A wailing cry from Ryan reverberates throughout the room, as he feels the other hand of the creature violently thrust itself into the upper left cavity of his chest, grasping a fistful of muscle. Drawing out the warm, pumping heart, the creature severs healthy ventricles and arteries from a six-foot Ryan, steam rising against the frigid air, sealing his fate.

Ryan drops the flashlight. The monster retracts the knife-like fingers from the cavity, and Ryan plummets effortlessly to the ground, splattering bright red all over the rock wall. A coagulated pond slowly forms around the lifeless human. Steam rises from the forming puddle against the frigid air. The light eventually goes dark on the man who hides his deepest secrets in the very space that has sealed his fate. The Task is now complete.

***

In the weeks that follow, officers discover the dismantled and desecrated body of Fredrick Ryan Robinson in the basement of the family property. The case makes national news, and officers are left without any explanation. No other case is comparable to the Robinson case. Shreds of rotten flesh are more than the experienced team of agents can handle. Every bone from the body is unrecovered, and all that remains are hair, nails, and skin. Organs are decomposed, the room swarming with flies. The case grows old with no leads after months of investigation. Ryan's private journal continues to remain an unknown secret to authorities and remains in a secret location unbeknownst to the family. What is left of Ryan's body is buried on the cabin property underneath a large walnut tree, and the cabin is closed off for the time being as the family grieves.

Renee's body was never recovered.

# Part II: Seeds

# Chapter 7

"It's hard to understand where this all began. I remember being a little boy, close to eight or nine, I would guess," Ryan begins. "There was this trip that my folks and I had taken up north to The Rockies. On our way back down the mountain, we made a turn down a winding road, and a large deer hurled itself into the front of our jeep. It happened so quickly that we all went into shock. None of us was hurt. My dad and I got out of the car and saw the deer barely scamper away, leaving a trail of blood behind. I could hear it making this dreadful cry for help, and I knew that it was dying. That image stuck with me for the rest of my life, and I believe that, at that moment, watching the animal's pain and suffering as it struggled to survive, ignited a fire of desire in me. I suddenly felt the desperate urge to murder. Something in the way it ran off made me angry, and I wanted to kill it. I was mad that it had stupidly hit our car and caused us the inconvenience of having to flag a stranger down on the side of a mountain. My mother stayed in the car and was crying out of sympathy." Ryan pauses. "I wanted to punch her in the fucking face."

The therapist pauses for a moment and looks down at her notepad in front of her. She takes a deep breath and replies, "Does your family ever go hunting?"

Ryan shakes his head, and with that, the session is over. He pops up and makes his way down the hall of his local middle school. He walks out front, glaring at his peers. He suspects they all know he just left his weekly therapy session.

The year is 2009.

The older kids gawk and whisper, "Freak," as Ryan makes his way out. Soon, a recognizable vehicle makes its way through the parking lot and stops right in front of the young seventh grader.

Ryan opens the passenger door, and his mom greets him. "Well, do you feel like you had a productive session, son?" Ryan doesn't respond and keeps his eyes on the group of boys nearby, who continue to laugh and stare in his direction. "I am sure you had the best time with Penny. She is wonderful, and everyone recommends her for life enrichment sessions. Why don't we get something to eat? I haven't eaten since earlier, and I am so hungry. Plus, I must get home and make your lunch for tomorrow. I know how much you love my homemade egg salad sandwiches with peanut butter. I might even throw in a slice of fruit cake for dessert." Ryan's mom continues to talk to herself for the entire fourteen-minute ride home. "We are going to your grandparents' home this weekend, so make sure you pack a small bag for two nights. Your father and I have a hotel booked for the two of us in town, so you'll be staying with Nanny and Papa," Ryan's mom, Grace, says.

That night, something deep inside of Ryan festers, and he reaches for his journal on the small bedside table. Turning on a small flashlight, he angrily writes in his book. The moonlight shines through his bedroom window, casting down narrow paths of light that makes him desperately want to go outside. Looking down at his latest entry, an exquisitely dictated drawing of a large body of skeleton bones stares back at him.

Throughout the night, Ryan continually stirs and struggles to find sleep. An eagerness sweeps over him. The young man is ready for his weekend getaway.

# Chapter 8

Driving down to the cabin is rather boring. Fields and small one-stoplight towns with a single gas pump are all that exist. It is a sixty-mile trip one way. The family makes the trip once or twice a year, typically in the summer and again around Christmas time. Ryan sleeps the entire way or stares out the window, daydreaming. The family seldom stops for snacks since Grace usually packs sandwiches. Coming into the border of a tall wall of woods, Ryan darts up from a slumber, knowing they are finally getting close. About ten minutes later, a small gravel driveway appears, as the shape of the small family cabin comes into view. A well with a crank sits off to the side, reminding Ryan of the countless times his grandmother yelled at him for fear of his falling in. A five-foot-tall elderly woman with a golden colored perm and perfectly starched pants waves down the slowing car from the front deck. She wears a floral button-down top, a staple of her wardrobe.

Ryan grabs his small duffle bag, hugs her, and runs straight to his room, in typical preteen fashion.

Ryan's room is down the small hall and to the left, next to the narrow door leading to the basement. Ryan turns the knob and studies the ten-by-ten-foot room; nothing has been touched in six months. Feeling a desperate need to hide himself from his family, he makes his way down to the basement to carry out his private plans. Turning on the light from the top of the stairs, he thoughtfully calculates the contents of the area.

The space is rather large. The walls are made of large stone rocks that date back over a hundred years. It is cold and damp. The smell of dirt penetrates his senses. He knows every square inch of the basement. From above, he hears his parents crank up the car and drift away. Not a single goodbye. His dad is probably already pulling out a flask from the console. His grandma is upstairs rattling pots and pans while his grandpa is probably off in the woods chopping down a tree for firewood.

Ryan retrieves a smaller backpack from the red and blue duffle. He hollers out from the basement stairs. "Grandma, I am going out into the woods. I will try to be home soon. Is that, okay?" He pauses at the threshold, listening for any signs of movement upstairs, but the house remains quiet except for the faint clatter of cookware. Ryan's heart thuds as he descends, each step echoing his anticipation and trepidation. The familiar chill of the basement wraps around him, grounding his swirling thoughts. He moves with purpose, searching through a pile of old boxes and rusty tools, making certain no one will disturb him. This is his sanctuary—where secrets can be kept and plans can be made without interference. Finally, a response.

"Well, how about you take some of this roast in a Tupperware, dear?" she says. "And take this lantern in case you stay out too long. And grab those matches by the door. Watch your steps in the leaves. Those copperheads will get you. You try to be home by ten."

Gleefully, Ryan heads up the stairs and snatches up the food and lantern and pockets the box of matches by the front door. Making his way down the stairs of the front deck, Ryan feels a surreal surge of power overcoming him. Leaving the driveway, the sensation of crunching gravel under his sneakers sends shrills of excitement through his shoulders and down his body. A gentle gust of pine-filled winds provides a certain comfort that the city never offers its residents. The leaves rustle as he makes his way deeper into the woods. His motions for the weekend are quickly falling into place. And he is ready.

Kneeling against a large fallen tree, Ryan removes the contents of his backpack. Pulling off the lid of the roast, he carefully takes small pieces and lays them out in separate piles around the fallen, dilapidated trunk. Setting aside the dish, he retrieves the small bag of rat poison from the basement and sprinkles the green granules over the freshly roasted beef. Gathering up his belongings, Ryan moves himself some fifty yards away and eagerly awaits. As daylight begins to succumb to the shadows of the night, he grows even more impatient with each minute that passes.

"Why the fuck are you taking so long?" he grumbles. Trying not to move or breathe too heavily, he realizes that if he were to turn on the lantern, he'd blow the entire stakeout. He makes the executive decision to head back, counting his steps along the way for an exact judgment of distance. He lights the handheld lantern approximately halfway back and eventually approaches the front deck of the cabin. Ryan has only been gone a few hours, pleasing his grandma with an early arrival. Tossing the empty Tupperware into the sink, he compliments his grandma on a job well done as he lets her know he will be heading back out first thing in the morning. She obliges.

Once in his room, he pulls out his journal and scribbles out a detailed visual. Looking out through the window and into the forest, Ryan feels the desperate urge to pry his hands into a frothy, warm flesh. The raging internal fire burns into his heart as uncontrollable adrenaline festers within. His hands begin to perspire salty drippings as his anger drives his body temperature up. He continues to daydream in his own world of impure thoughts. With nothing left to do at this point, he waits—all night.

Hours.

Taking a step back, forcing himself to perceive this in a unique way, he realizes this must be the way boys his age daydream about girls in his class. He turns the thought repeatedly over in his mind for a few moments before turning his face down to view the number he has written on the page.

1,488.

That is the number of steps. In a matter of hours, he'd recant the number while plodding through the deep Texas woods.

# Chapter 9

A well-worn pair of sneakers beat aggressively into the crunching earth below. Soaking in every ounce of freedom, Ryan forms an unassailable relationship with the woods while alone with his private thoughts and desires. A racing heart forcefully pushes hot surges of blood throughout the approximately six thousand feet of veins found in the young boy's body. Steady counting continues. "Seven-hundred-eighty-eight… 789, 790… The faster, the better!" Ryan coaches himself. The morning air and sweet, dewy scent of the woods feed a swift and gallant race to meet Ryan's overnight aim. Various birds and squirrels shoot off in different directions, hinting at a need for safety. Legs and lungs burn as he approaches close to 1,400 steps, forcing himself to a slow pace into the center of the forest. HIS forest. Creeping closer, Ryan crouches down, almost replicating a predatory stance, hunting his prey. Making calculated rounds of the large trunk, he discovers that five of the nine mounds of food have been tampered with, igniting a hot flame inside of him. Instincts at once kick in as he surveys the area.

He is on the hunt.

Scouring the perimeter of partially eaten roast with death sprinkles, Ryan adamantly scurries through the woods searching for any remnants of life. In one direction, probably southeast, an opossum lay effortlessly on the leaves, its tail coiled on its left side, feet curled inward. It makes small, pitiful sounds of desperation as he eases over the soon-to-be corpse.

Breathing transitions to a shallow gasp as Cheyne-Stokes begins to develop in the small rodent. Death courses through its veins like the flood of a bar ditch from a week's worth of storms. Blackened eyes emptily stare straight forward into a nothingness, as the beautifully grey and white patterned animal draws in its final breath of air. Its chest completely deflates one last time in acceptance. Its tiny, sharp, white teeth show in a mouth that stays gaping. Looking overhead, Ryan notices three large vultures circling the realm of trees, challenging Ryan for the carcass first. Without hesitation, he gathers the lifeless body and places it in a black, thirty-gallon trash bag, as he resumes his hunt.

Ryan detects an unfamiliar spirit surrounding him. The spirit is dark and unearthly. He welcomes the new sensation as it envelops his soul, ever so passionately. A heavy cloud forms over the area, darkening everything in sight. The air cools to a chilling breeze that sends shivers over Ryan's body. He sucks in the air, visualizing an entity creeping through his veins.

The young killer looks down upon the dead opossum in the black bag. He runs his hands down the course of the animal's body, leaving stunning ribbons of grey and white in the fur. The warmth of the body dissipates within minutes, and the body hardens as Ryan continues his search of the area for further trophies. A diabolical tunnel vision takes over as Ryan's view turns grim.

Several hours later, a total of eight carcasses had been collected within a quarter-mile range; necks forcibly broken with bare hands since some were still breathing. Ryan, in a rage, punches one of the animals in the face as it valiantly fights back to run free. In all, the largest animal awarded is a young fawn. In a mad race against time, the animals are skinned, strung up on the highest limb in reach, their muscles and flesh torn apart with bare hands. Bones are easily snapped purely through adrenaline and set aside to roast over a small fire built in the cupped earth. Ryan eats most of his kill, some cooked, some raw. Multiple smells infiltrate the space as the fire tries to mask the cooking flesh.

Only thirteen years old, Ryan now knows the thrill of a lifetime and recognizes his power. "This is better than any girl at school. Fuck that," he proclaims.

Ryan's mind ventures into deeper realms of curiosity. The flesh of larger animals, such as a raw bobcat or a wild dog, piques his interest. Shreds of bloody tissue caress his teeth and trigger umami, leading him to ravage the dead animals in no discernible amount of time. The taste and feel of moist meat satisfy every craving in every aspect. Power and strength divulge hundreds of pores as he feels a practical sense of life overtakes him. Realizing the amount of time and work he has ingested, Ryan hastily wraps up his workplace over the next thirty minutes and sets off in the fastest sprint he has ever done. In record time, he makes it home just as dinner is pulled from the vintage oven.

His grandmother has spent the past several hours preparing a rack of ribs she purchased at the nearest town farmer's market a few days prior. She has also prepared a large crock pot of creamy, mashed red potatoes with sour cream and chives, all doused in a rich brown gravy. The ribs had been slowly smoked, and the smell is to die for. Washing off the dried blood from his arms and hands, Ryan realizes that not a single drop of blood tattered his apparel. It is another achievement for the boy. Donning a fresh set of pajamas, Ryan makes his way down the hall and into the main room of the cabin. His grandparents greet him with a multitude of questions. Ryan regales his two elders on his voyage through the murky woods. Ryan, vaguely giving each question, absconds his inner secrecy and shrugs off most of their curiosities as they dish out the lovingly prepared meal before them.

The small trio bow their heads, take each other's hands, and recite a small prayer. Rising heads view the beautiful candlelit setting as their faces turn to their plates and devour their servings. A generously filled plate that every teenage boy could crave lay before Ryan as he forces a smile upon it.

His stomach wrenches in disgust over the elaborate sight as he watches his two grandparents soak up every morsel on their plates. Striving fiercely to control his stomach, Ryan pushes vomit down to keep the lives of his victims inside of him. He makes eye contact with each grandparent as they subtly question his sudden lack of appetite.

He is not hungry.

# Chapter 10

*Six months later.*

Following the festivities at school, the Robinson family wraps up their shopping and packs their gifts for a family Christmas celebration fifty miles away at the cabin. The hustling of a city-wide community is enough to invite the small family to the hidden wilderness of Texas, where peace is easily proven. Disregarding neighborhood invitations and get-togethers, their souls are called to join the isolated cabin. Being the only child of Bob and Grace Robinson, Ryan is the gift they had prayed for over a decade prior. The couple tried several times after Ryan's first birthday to have one more child, which turned out unsuccessfully, leaving Grace in a period of depression. Over the years, the young mother realized it was a blessing to have one son.

Trying his best not to trigger a means of "necessary life enrichment therapy" with an intimidated young Penny, Ryan sets up a grand facade, pretending to admire the most intelligent coeds in his grade, to appear as a normal teen to his parents. Following the paths of his popular male acquaintances at school, Ryan decides to take internal notes on how to sway and elevate his status in his high school social circle. Realizing how hard it is to try to fit in, he urgently craves his privacy in the woods. Every thought about school evaporates his brain as nerve endings shoot signals and desires, leaving him in a raging obsession. Grasping a nearby afghan blanket in the seat next to him, he quietly pulls it over his lap as thoughts of warm flesh invade his mind. Ryan's dad continues to make his way down the highway as the winter darkness covers the family vehicle. Mom is passed out in the front seat, as Dad gently turns the volume knob upwards on the local radio station. Christmas music fills the air. Ryan gently leans his head over to remove his reflection from the rearview mirror.

Pulling down the zipper of his pants, he slowly wedges his erect penis free from the garment as he envisions small warm bodies over him. Within minutes, warm cum secretes itself from the head of his penis as an intense orgasm sends powerful thrills throughout his body. His deep breathing is muffled into the rhythmic beats of the music sounding through the car. A cold sweat clams up his forehead and drenches his upper body underneath his sweater. Heavily relaxed, he opens his eyes to see the mile marker on the highway. It signals the halfway mark, and with that, Ryan begins to jerk off once more, sending another surge of hot cum over his abdomen. The musty smell wells up from his groin, so he pulls his boxer briefs over the cum, and scrapes it down over his perineal area, hiding all evidence. Forcing himself to accept the cold saturation on himself, he sucks inward and zips up his pants. He draws in a deep sense of relief as his father continues to talk to himself from the front seat, not knowing a single detail of the perversion his son just took in.

The family eases into the cabin in a darkness that continues to instill sleepiness, calling them to a fresh set of linens underneath a hand-stitched quilt over each awaiting bed. The fireplace inside provides the perfect amount of warmth to cancel out a twenty-milligram dose of melatonin. The crackles and pops of the twigs and limbs from outside are more welcoming to the ears than that of any small talk.

"Young man, you are not to go out tomorrow. The air is enough to catch the flu, and we can't have that right now. You disobey me and I'll bust your ass clean against the skin with the belt. You hear me?" His dad's stern announcement sends a rush of tension in the air as the family quiets. Each person retreats to their own lodgings for the night, all tired.

The time is 11:55 PM.

Ryan's grandfather decides to toss a couple more logs into the iron stove, ensuring a warm night ahead. Stoking the fire, he shuts the door to the stove and lays down the poker on the hearth he had built years earlier. His bones crack as he carefully lifts himself from the main room floor. The drapes are drawn to encapsulate the warmth from the winter's frigid temperatures outside. It is a fight that everyone faces this time of year.

The grandfather clock in the living room sets off a distinctive jingle signifying the midnight hour. The fire in the living room continues to provide a generous blanket of heat, which shines an amber glow through the cracks of the iron, showing its tremendous temperatures. The cabin is eerily quiet until two single footsteps creep down the hall, sending painfully loud creaking sounds throughout the main room and into the kitchen. With any hope, they can easily be transposed to the sounds of the fire. The sounds alarm a timid Ryan as he recoils and trembles his way through the small home, fearing his father coming down the hall to swing the leather belt against him, buckle first. Feeling brave enough to try the front door, he gathers his prepared bag hidden behind the burlap sack of potatoes in the pantry. The backpack is frocked with cold cuts of turkey and ham, which have been warming up inside the bag he had prepacked earlier. He gently grabs one of the oil-filled lanterns, which has a small satchel tied to the handle and plenty of matches inside. Gently grasping the knob and glancing back inside the warm home, he opens the door. Writhing inside, he successfully makes his way outside into bitter cold temperatures. Looking back at the draped windows, knowing his family is cozy in their warm beds, he recants his father's orders. His urge for power and curiosity continues to flood his every sense.

"I'm the fucking boss of me," Ryan proclaims under his breath. Ryan sets off into the depths of the woods, a terrain that he has lusted over for the past six months. "Fuck the counseling. Fuck the parents. Fuck the whole school and fuck the freezing weather. And fuck you, Dad, you drunk asshole. All you've ever done is put yourself first. And the bottle," he announces to himself. "I'm my own person, and I will make my way through this life. I will be respected. I will be powerful." Ryan continues further into the desolate forest.

Enduring the bitter cold of the night air, Ryan takes in one sharp breath after the next, as each sears his upper chest. His nose progressively drains, causing the snot to freeze on his face. With every step, Ryan continues to separate himself from the cabin. The dark, desolate woods send fear throughout his body as he hears popping and cracking all around him. Gusts of winter air force multiple limbs crashing to the ground. He forces himself to go deeper into the woods, despite branches clipping and snagging at his attire. The moonlight cast shadows of eerie movements here and there. Wild animals hibernate during this time of year, and this truth causes rage to flare up inside him, knowing they would be hard to find. Setting aside the pros and cons of his mission, he presses on.

Arriving at the core of the forest, Ryan delicately lays out the cold cuts of meat.

He is not alone. Sensing a heavy presence nearby, Ryan stops all movement and listens intently. Cries ring out through the echoing woods with nothing to buffer them. Every single leaf is on the earth's floor, allowing the terrifying screams to penetrate the ears for what feels like miles. The screams are not of any wild animal that he knows of. Cowering down into a nearby rock formation, Ryan suddenly feels a wave of regret come over him. A battle inside of him develops as the human-like screams continue to echo all around him.

*"POP, POP, POP!!"* The popping sound is not tree limbs breaking. There is no crash that follows.

*"AHHHHH!!"* Deadly wails continue to permeate the air as Ryan realizes they are most definitely coming from a human. The popping sound is the breaking of bones, followed by painful bellowing in a desperate plea for help. Then, out of nowhere, the screams come to a sudden stop. Not a single sound is made for over five minutes. Frozen to the same spot near the rock formation, Ryan fears he is next. Something is out in the pitch-black woods waiting patiently.

Using all his energy, Ryan falls asleep in an upright position and doesn't wake up for another hour. Ryan freezes, barely able to peek over the jagged edge of the rock. His heart thunders in his chest, each beat threatening to give away his hiding spot. Shadows flicker past, cast by the trembling lantern light he clings to. For a brief moment, he thinks he sees a hunched figure moving between the trees—too large, too lopsided to be any animal he knows. The presence is suffocating, chilling him deeper than the sharp wind ever could. Ryan squeezes his eyes shut, silently pleading for the creature to pass him by, for the forest to swallow all memory of what he's witnessed.

***

Waking from a deep slumber, Ryan's eyes open to a spread of woods before him. Jolting upright, Ryan suddenly remembers the point of his mission. Feeling as though he had a terrible dream, Ryan brushes the thoughts from his mind as he focuses on the meat he had packed. After an hour has passed without any animals showing interest in the turkey and ham, he puts on gloves as dusk approaches and uses a small shovel he brought earlier that evening to dig the deepest hole he can. He continues to work at the fresh soil until the sun begins to rise through the tree line. He leaves his items against the familiar fallen trunk and bolts to the cabin, arriving through the back door as his father exits through the front. It is perfect timing.

Breaking down his father with his annoying teenage antics, Ryan returns for no more than six hours at a time each day over the two-week Christmas holiday to remove the Texas soil from the earth's crust. The teen builds a four-foot-deep, fourteen-foot-long bed as planned in his journal. Stepping away from the bed, he pulls each fingertip of his gloves, removing them to expose two diligently wrapped hands in cloth. Ryan unwinds the sweat-drenched cloth and looks down at a perfectly intact pair of hands, free of blisters. His pride runs deep. Planning everything accordingly allows Ryan to feel a sense of accomplishment as he regains his strength and mentality. Lowering himself down into the bed, he precisely constructs the hundreds of bones with a painstaking amount of patience. Several hours pass before he takes a deep breath and leans back into the dirt wall. His shoulders and neck ache so badly from keeping the same position. Rubbing his face in a massaging gesture, he climbs to his feet and pulls himself from the hole. Stepping back in utter shock, Ryan evaluates his formation, his jaw dropping.

Before him presents an enormous, hand-crafted structure with such intricate detailing that it is almost too good to be true. Starting from the top of the "head," Ryan gazes over the artifact, studying it. Tufts of fur from various animals adorn the skeletal structure as if it is ready to go on display. Long, stencil-like fingers cascade over the torso, as legs so incredibly strong lead to two large hooves collected from a pasture out west. The finding makes Ryan proud. Standing back to admire his creation, he instantly feels a connection below. Each individual bone resembles a part of a life he took…and tasted. The fresh meat of the dead carcasses now thrives within his soul. They are a part of him now.

Walking to the dilapidated tree, Ryan retrieves his journal and tears out five sheets of thoughts and desires. Lovingly, he places the sheets over the bones of his creation and weeps uncontrollably as the papers collect his tears. Sucking back snot and pushing down his emotions, he realizes he only has two days left before his family heads back home and resumes their everyday life. Anger washes over him as he masturbates urgently to his impure thoughts. Cum shoots over the creation and lands on the papers and bones. Gathering himself, Ryan takes a step back and grabs his shovel. He recants a language not of this earth and looks to the sky as dark clouds form overhead. Shoveling mounds of dirt and roots, Ryan covers his creature and says goodbye.

****

Ryan spends the last two days of his vacation retreating to his place of refuge in the woods, soaking up every possible source of life. The young man's creation is buried and preserved under the cold soil, encapsulated in his journal entries that elaborate heartfelt symphonies of demonic power. Ryan wants so desperately to feel his creation. He wants to touch it. And he longs to cherish every possible part. As time ends, he writes one more letter and lays it atop the mound of soil covering a new force of life.

The young man makes the trek towards the cabin, envisioning the drive back home. A newfound sensation of penetrating sorrow bellows within. If his family decides to adhere to their customary schedule, visiting during the summer and Christmas holidays, it would be six months before he could pay his respects at the grave. Ryan gathers his strength and buries it deep within to prepare for an unknown future.

Unbeknownst to him, he will not return until many years later, when he is a grown adult.

# Chapter 11

Over the course of Ryan's high school years, the family suffers many detrimental challenges as both of his grandparents endure the onset of dementia. The middle-aged Grace, alongside her spouse, Bob, turns their focus on the elderly couple and is forced to move them into a nursing home. Holidays turn glum as Ryan grows with each forthcoming year as a typical teen whose future appears bright and promising. His grades are more than scholarly as universities turn their heads his way. Ultimately, the Robinson family migrates to a new rotation of life, and the cabin becomes a distant memory, buried deep within Ryan's soul. This new disposition enables the up-and-coming leader of the community to stand out amongst the crowd.

Over time, Ryan forms a close group of friends that boosts his popularity and helps him develop leadership skills. His dark humor provides a subtle yet dry sarcasm that proves his role of stature. Some find him to be intimidating, while others want to be him. His parents give him a new BMW Coupe for his sixteenth birthday, screaming extravagant dollar signs each morning as he pulls into the school parking lot.

No one fucks with him.

As the years pass and high school ends, Ryan enters a time in his life where his 4.4 GPA locks his status in the community. College swiftly arrives and extracurricular activities consume Ryan's spare time, alongside his social congregation. Ryan chooses the direction of education, focusing on something that he thinks will never bore him. He is wrong. After two years of college, his education becomes stagnant for him, and he quickly loses his trajectory on things that matter.

Partial journal entries are made in complete and utter privacy. Elaborate notes cascade each page of a leatherbound journal detailing the ongoing hills and valleys of a persistent yearning for death. Ryan periodically feels physical urges as he tries to ignore his desire for more. More hearts. More blood. More bodies.

***

Ryan, living off campus in a top-floor apartment, struggles to concentrate on a lengthy report due in three days. Frustrated, he gazes out his bedroom window at the university, visible from his vantage point. The apartment complex consists of two-story buildings arranged around a pool for residents. He tries to unwind by tossing back a shot of whiskey, but the neighbor's dog won't stop barking, driving him further up the wall. In exasperation, Ryan throws his pencil across the room and goes next door to knock, only to find no one home after waiting a full minute. Through the torn blinds, he notices the anxious dog inside.

Forced to endure the constant howling, Ryan returns to his apartment and storms down the hallway. He enters the guest room, opens the closet door, draws the curtains, and pulls a chair into the closet. Removing a white piece of wood from the ceiling, he climbs into the attic crawlspace. Wearing only boxer briefs and shoes wrapped in grocery bags to conceal any evidence, he heads toward the entrance above his neighbor's closet and carefully lifts the board. Ryan whistles softly, prompting the sound of trotting paws. Shadows flicker as a full-grown Siberian Husky appears beneath the opening. He retrieves a snack bag from his waistband, puts on latex gloves, and offers the dog a ball of peanut butter after practicing some quick hand motions. The eager yet growling Husky sits obediently and devours the treat in one gulp. Ryan replaces the board, climbs down from the attic, and at once showers. He throws his boxers into a hot wash and disposes of the gloves and bags separately in a small trash receptacle several buildings down.

Coming back inside, Ryan casually pours whiskey on the rocks and turns on a soft jazz instrumental as he resumes his report in solace.

Almost forgetting, he nonchalantly lets out, "Oh, darn, ha-ha…. I *almost* forgot!" Laughingly, Ryan gets up from his seated position at his desk and takes his glass of whiskey with him. He dances over to the kitchen counter and sets the whiskey on it. He retrieves the pack of lithium-ion button batteries he had left out and places them back in the kitchen junk drawer.

The next-door neighbors return home later that evening. After a brief commotion and the closing of the front door, Ryan remains at his desk undisturbed, allowing him to continue his studies in a calm environment thereafter.

It is later that Ryan overhears a phone conversation through the walls of the apartment surrounding the details of the Husky's near death. Turning everything off in his apartment, Ryan listens intently to the conversation. "It was a button battery, Mom. He swallowed one and it ate through his insides. The vet said if untreated after some time, its fatal."

A quiet laugh escapes Ryan as he, filled with pride, makes plans to spend the evening with his friends.

***

Suppressing his past, the young man finally graduates with honors from college. After a matchmade date by mutual friends, Renee agrees to a date with Ryan. The pair fell instantly for each other after a quiet night of deep conversation at a local pub. Ryan, who never looked into dating, found the young redhead intriguing and sweet. Her soft laugh replenished his spirit, sending his heart and mind into a wave of fierce love and passion. He adored her. As time went on, the couple became a stunning image to friends and family. Everyone approved and accepted them.

A young Renee in tow, unknowingly masks his deceptive motives as she quite nicely compliments the young man. It is the ideal image. The couple buys a home near their alumni on prestigious Maple Street. Neighbors shower them with baked goods, potted plants, and handmade cards, making them feel welcome.

Noisy barking, catfights, and frequent piles of animal waste disturb Ryan's nights and ruin his lawn with an unpleasant odor that draws flies.

Ryan purchases a lengthy amount of zapping wire that shocks anything coming in or out of his perimeter. It isn't enough. Hurdling over each wire, the cats and dogs continue to outsmart him. Losing his temper, Ryan formulates a new course of action against the incessant nuisances of the neighborhood.

One day, while walking off the back porch of his meticulously landscaped yard, Ryan spots an adult squirrel that somehow wedged itself between two pieces of fencing. Severely annoyed, Ryan looks at the helpless critter and instantly bends its entire head backwards, slowly snapping its neck in half. Gradual action causes noticeable pain throughout its body as it twitches into a motionless state.

The Hollow

Gazing into the black eyes of the lifeless animal between his bare hands, Ryan casually slings it over the fence line and into the neighbor's backyard. The brown-haired animal flies in a circular motion, its arms and legs sticking straight out as if it were a Frisbee. It splatters on the concrete patio directly in front of the glass-paned doors to the home, creating a ghastly sight.

Peeking through the blinds of the side room in Ryan's home, he straightens his stance in alarm as his next-door neighbor, a woman, approximately sixty years of age, comes home and steps directly into the blood spatter on her back porch.

Ryan, enthralled with excitement, eagerly retreats to the back patio with a whiskey on the rocks, convulsing so hard with laughter that he can barely contain his volume. He relishes as the stuck-up bitch with a pole up her ass lets out a ridiculous, high-pitched shriek that can be heard from the next street over. Finding a heartwarming attraction to the mortified heifer, Ryan continues to listen as she orders her annoyed husband to call animal control to remove the dead carcass from their patio.

In the next hour, Ryan excitedly devises a plan that sets him off on a delightful new conquest through his community. A remarkable venture awaits the young man as he continues to sip his whiskey, a vindictive smile spreading ear to ear. Ryan admires the sun falling over the Texas skyline, creating shards of pinks and purples as if it were a painting on canvas. Renee joins him outside with a glass of bubbling champagne. It is the couple's first wedding anniversary. The duo toasts to one year of milestones and accomplishments as they enjoy the beautiful sunset.

Ryan relives the soaring squirrel in his mind and subtly lets out a "Weeee!" as their glasses clink together in the evening air.

# Chapter 12

Arriving back home from a golf outing with coworkers, Ryan comes through the front door and leans on the inside of the kitchen doorway. Staring at the back of her head, Ryan laughingly says, "Your hair is all kinds of cattywampus."

Smiling, Renee replied, "It's not easy being this pretty!" Ryan watches as Renee removes the shriveled-up morsels of jerky from a large hollow dehydrator. The home is filled with aromas of savory garlic and tang that Renee loves. Ryan precut and prepared the strands the night before, marinating them in a special recipe that his mother used growing up. Each home always has a specialty they would make in bulk. The Robinsons always choose beef jerky.

Ryan goes on. "Hey, I saw the Kensington's Maine Coon dart behind the car when I pulled into the neighborhood. The big guy just keeps us all on our toes."

"Well, they need to start putting trackers on their pets with everything that keeps happening. It must be a coyote or bobcat coming in from the woods down south. Too many babies are going missing. Well, why don't you run this over to them fast? Let them know he's still zooming around here," Renee says.

"Will do." Ryan grabs the small woven basket, makes his way out the front door, and walks down the sidewalk. Approaching a three-story home, adorned with impeccable landscaping, he treks up a glamorous flight of stairs that leads to twelve-foot double doors. Before he could press his finger to the doorbell, Mr. Kensington answers swiftly, seemingly stressed out.

"Oh, hey Ryan," he says, looking somewhat confused.

"Renee and I wanted to bring these by to you. We know how hard it's been with Cooper missing and all. I saw him outside the back wall of the neighborhood before I pulled into the gate. He's still out there," Ryan ensures.

Mr. Kensington takes the basket holding five medium-sized bags of jerky—enough to last them about a week or so. He sets the basket on the entryway table and replies, "We appreciate you folks so much. I'm going to go take a walk now and see if I can find him. We'll see you soon, Ryan. Thanks for the heads up."

With that, the two part ways, and Ryan makes his way back toward the house, turning his head to view Mr. Kensington jet off down the street, leash and collar in hand. Ryan laughs to himself as he watches the young neighbor take off in a desperate attempt to retrieve the small animal.

Stepping back onto the porch, Ryan paused for a moment, glancing up at the dusky sky as the cicadas began their evening chorus. The neighborhood felt tense, and a quiet unease had settled in with the recent string of disappearances. He let out a slow breath, the weight of what he'd done simmering beneath the surface, masked by his practiced calm. The air was thick with summer heat, carrying with it the faint scent of grilled meat and cut grass, blending innocently with the secrets he now bore.

Entering the home, Ryan notices that Renee has made up all the fancy little jerky bags, placing them into different small baskets that adorn the island in the kitchen. Each basket holds a little handwritten note and is topped with a burlap bow for decoration. She is now drinking tea on the couch and listening to the local news report on TV, not realizing he has returned.

Ryan slowly and quietly eases his way to the back of the house and slips into the back room, where a large, deep freezer holds hundreds of dollars' worth of stored food. Opening the lid, he takes in the left side of the freezer where approximately thirty packages of meat lay. All wrapped in a white butcher paper; they are the same paper provided by their local butcher. Running his hands in a stroking motion over the freezing white paper, he suddenly feels his penis erect against his polyester golfing slacks.

From a distant background, Ryan hears the reporter on the television state, "And that makes approximately thirteen cases of reported missing pets in this part of the community. Robin, back to you." Ryan gently closes the lid to the freezer and walks to the bathroom to run his shower. The glass doors of the shower rapidly fog up. He envisions the missing pets from the news report on television as he presses his left palm to the wall underneath the spraying shower head. Stroking his penis with a soft, soapy sponge in his right hand, he masturbates underneath the steaming water, orgasming in under sixty seconds.

Cooper, the Kensington's giant Maine Coon, is still around. Ryan has made sure of that. Unbeknownst to Renee, with her sincere generosity of savory jerky-filled baskets, Cooper's owners will now have their precious pet inside of them for the rest of their lives.

The date is August 11th.

Within twenty-four hours, the community's local animal predator will be unmasked.

# Part III: The Hole

# Chapter 13

*"Never underestimate the importance of the beginning. Of anything. The beginning has the seeds of everything else to come." -Carolyn Coman, The Memory Bank*

April 1984, Lake Conroe, Texas

An elderly man in a black suit walks into a nearby gas station and bait shop to relieve himself in the men's restroom. After some time, a line forms in the cluttered hallway outside the restroom door. The line grows to a heightened desperation as two of the men storm to the woods behind the shop to drain their bladders.

Almost in tears, a boy around the age of twelve trembles for fear of pissing himself in front of the tourists and fishermen. A store manager is notified and retrieves the keys to check on the old man.

Just before the key enters the silver handle, the man finally comes out and angrily looks over the small crowd.

Cursing at the gathering before him, he angrily states, "Can't a fucking man have some privacy!" He waves his hands in people's faces as he passes through the crowd, exiting the shop.

A young gentleman retorts to himself and looks down at the trembling boy. "Dude, go first."

The preteen rushes inside, not locking the door, rips down his jeans, and lets out a full sixty seconds of urine, his eyes closed in relief. Taking in a deep sigh, he flushes the toilet and looks down. The old man had dropped what appeared to be a large silver coin. The boy picks it up from the floor and washes the coin in the sink as he washes his own hands. He pockets the coin and exits the bait store, looking for his parents' brand-new Pontiac Parisienne wagon.

In the gravel parking lot, various cars and trucks with small fishing boats are askew throughout the area. Spring is in full force as the southeastern Texas heat is becoming clear. Covering his eyes with his right hand to block out the glare of the sun, the boy spots the wagon across the lot and walks towards it. Out of nowhere, the old man blocks the boy's mission halfway and glares straight into his eyes. The boy stops dead in his tracks and comes face to face with the man, who lets out a string of profanities under his breath.

"You fucking little bastard. I know what you have, you thieving son of a bitch. Give it back to me if you want to live, you little shit."

The boy feels a fire burn on his side, knowing the coin is hiding there. A wave of power surges through him as he cracks a devilish grin and mockingly states, "Finders, keepers, losers, weepers."

Taken aback, the man looks at him and relinquishes what was once his. He feels relief come over him and watches the boy stomp off, his head held high. The old man mutters to himself as he looks to the sky above and retreats to his vehicle. The two part ways and never see each other again.

Monday follows the eventful weekend, and the small trio heads back to their family cabin in the woods. The boy begins his normal school week at the local middle school, approximately six miles from their home. Finding the only time to head to the library, the boy grabs an apple for lunch and eats it as he pulls each drawer to flip through the card catalog in search of a book of symbols. Landing on two different book titles, the boy writes down the call numbers for each title and turns them into an elderly woman with short, iron-curled red hair. She sports a tied silk scarf around her neck along with a silk buttoned blouse which is neatly tucked into a wool pencil skirt. Her reading glasses are attached to a gold chain, ensuring their placement.

Looking down at his particular selection, she watches as he signs his name and hands him the books in their usual paper sack.

That evening, the boy sits on his bed and thumbs through the pages, looking for any similarities that show on the coin. He has seen nothing like it, and he knows there has to be something special about it or the old man wouldn't have wanted it back so badly. Tiny, delicate symbols wrap the perimeter of the silver, with the head of a goat centered in the detailing. The coin doesn't have a year of production on it; however, even to the young boy, its old age is clear. Finding similar styles, his interest peaks as a new realm of satanic idealism. From what he can read, the coin has existed for at least one hundred years. Writing down all pertinent information, the boy closes his books and returns to the library the following day, once again skipping his lunch.

Turning in the two books on symbols, he draws the card catalog from the wall and flips through the "D" and the "S" sections, writing down several call numbers. Setting his stack on the counter, the same librarian from the previous day sees its contents and snobbishly retorts, "Three books maximum!"

Pissed off, the impish boy scrutinizes her up and down and takes the first three. "Fine," He responds.

Her mannerisms grow increasingly impolite for a professional such as her. Taking note of his selections, she tactlessly withholds the standard bag from his books and turns away to the back room without saying a single word. Listening as the library door slams behind the boy, she heedlessly takes the remaining stack and pitches them in the metal trash can.

After a fury-filled afternoon in class, the boy arrives home and devours all three books in an expeditious amount of time, taking pages upon pages of notes. A glowing orange sun falls over the home as he relishes the newfound information overnight.

The next day, he skips lunch in the cafeteria again to head back to the library. The same librarian takes immense pride as she hatefully informs him that the remaining books on the devil and Satan are "unlocated indefinitely." The red-haired librarian smirks directly at him and he realizes this is premeditated on her part. Defeated, he resentfully leaves, while the austere woman watches his every step in sheer triumph.

***

Later that weekend, the family retreats to a new spot at Lake Conroe and selects a wooded site to camp. The lake is increasing in popularity each weekend as the temperatures rise and summer eases its way into the southern part of the state. Texas is home to numerous lakes, rivers, and reservoirs that families and fishermen camp for full weeks or weekends at a time. Ice chests and tents drape the banks, and the smell of fire and smoked fish fills the air. Vintage transistor radios play local music stations as kids play badminton, catch a baseball in their gloves, or toss a football around. The men usually drink their choice of beer and talk sports, while the women gossip and prepare meals for everyone.

Making his way down one of the many trails of the wooded forest, the boy carries a compass, a knapsack, and the coin. He ventures off for what seems like hours, coming up upon another campsite flocked with tourists. Looking ahead, an older man and woman are setting up their tents and tables for the weekend. The duo makes conversation with what appears to be friends they know. As the woman turns, the sun captures a gleam of her tresses, emitting a fiery red color that could be seen from a far-off distance. In an instant, a rage of adrenaline pierces the boy's veins. The librarian looks so happy, as if she carries out her life without giving a second thought about anyone else. Looking down at his compass, the boy notes his direction and makes his way back to his campsite, his frustrations growing along the way.

About halfway back, he decides to take a small break and sits down on a boulder just off the trail. Taking out the coin from his knapsack, he turns it repeatedly in his hands, contemplating life. Out of the corner of his eye, he sees movement and turns his head at once to lock eyes with a slithering Timber rattlesnake. Alarmed, the boy panics as he realizes he is only a few feet away from the approximately three-foot-long snake. The snake fixates in its place and tastes the air with a flick of its tongue. Thinking on a whim, he conjures a quick plan in his head and takes a nearby stick and coerces the snake into his knapsack. Adrenaline pounds throughout his arms and thighs, realizing he has successfully captured a venomous killer. Taking a smaller stick, he winds the top of the knapsack into a locking method he once read about, confining the snake within the cloth bag. He carries it back to his family's campsite, places the entire bag in a tote, and locks the lid. He retrieves his dad's switchblade and stabs several holes in the side for ventilation. Masking the tote under a lightweight blanket in his personal tent, he resumes the rest of his night at the lake with his parents and their newfound friends.

***

The crackling embers of the deteriorating fire emit a somewhat peaceful buffer to those who are still awake and have to listen to snoring in the midnight air. From a nearby tent, moans echo through the night, piercing the twelve-year-old's ears as he lies wide awake in his sleeping bag. As the moaning from a couple, several tents away, escalates, he begins to feel an erection form in his boxers.

Stroking his hardened penis, he masturbates as the gentle moaning turns into harsh sounds. As the couple's moaning and the masturbation escalates, the boy lustfully envisions what he would want in a woman- a young blonde with massive breasts—nipples turned upwards—riding a painfully thick dick, rubbing her clitoris against his right thumb as he massages her, creating the climax she desires.

As the moaning turns even more aggressive, the man vigorously turns her over and fucks her from behind, groping her hard nipples in the cool, night air. Taking his other hand, the man grabs a handful of hair and pulls straight backwards in a domineering fashion. Feeling the head of his penis rub against the saturated ridges of her vagina, he begins to press harder and faster, sending him into a convulsing orgasm, ejaculating straight inside of her. Grabbing her butt with both hands, he leaves bruises on her cheeks as he continues to pulsate inside of her. She lets out a scream of pain inside her pillow to muffle the sound.

Letting out a long sigh of relief, he pulls his wet penis out from her and falls onto the pallet next to her… The boy wipes his ejaculation and puts himself away in his boxers. Donning a fresh set of clothes, he prepares himself for the trek through the dark woods.

Inebriated adults pack almost every single tent at Lake Conroe, allowing the young couple to fuck each other in peace. Surprisingly, they are the only ones taking part that night. Gently unzipping his tent, feeling a sense of relief, the boy appears onto the path, waiting to turn on the small flashlight until he diminishes far into the woods. Lightly jogging down the path, he clenches the sealed knapsack away from his body and gropes the flashlight in the other. Sticks and leaves crunch underneath his shoes as he pounds his way down the path. A gentle breeze flows through the trees. An owl lets out several hoots nearby. Gentle rustles of brush in the woods surround him, reminding him that he is not alone.

Coming upon a familiar opening in the woods, he slows his pace to a soft tiptoe and turns off the flashlight as he approaches the campsite. Every single tent is dark inside, and similar fires are now going out, leaving only illuminated hot coals in the pits. Carefully inching his way towards the tent, he listens intently as he detects two distinct snores coming from inside, signaling two sleeping occupants. Running his semen-crusted fingers down the zipper line of the tent, he finally lands upon the cold metal tab of the zipper, finding it at the base of the tent. Annoyed by himself, he desperately rubs off the dried semen from his fingers before he slowly unzips the tent, leaving only three inches open.

Meticulously unwinding the stick to the knapsack, the boy gently takes the top of the bag and forces it through the opening at the base of the tent, using the stick to guide it. Not a single rattle is detected. Lightly touching his hand to the bag's bulk, the boy gently presses on it as it deflates, the contents transferring to their new location. As the weight evaporates from the bag, the boy grabs the bottom of the bag with his right hand and pulls it back, tugging the zipper down at the same time. Trotting into the woods nearby, he crouches down in the exact spot where he previously eyed the red-haired librarian hours earlier.

Several minutes pass by. Nothing is heard.

Growing impatient, the boy's anxiety kicks in, fearing he will be caught. Standing up from his crouched position, he begins his way back to his campsite. An overwhelming cry startles him from a distance. Screams turn into bursts of panic from nearby campers as the entire site rises to figure out what is happening.

A woman with bright red hair screams, "I'VE BEEN BITTEN! IT BURNS!!! IT BURNS!!!! SOMEONE HELP ME!" The husband, in a state of shock, has no idea how to help as he watches his wife transcend into anaphylactic shock. Her respirations slow while her immune system struggles to combat the hemotoxins. Not having access to a nearby phone, several adults race to their vehicles and take off down the main road in search of medical aid. A fellow camper produces a shovel as a small team of men finds the rattler inside the tent, separating its head from the rest of its body.

The boy races through the woods, tripping over a large limb in the pathway that wasn't there earlier. A cut presents itself on his right knee, trickling warm blood down his leg and into his shoe. Returning to his personal tent, the boy collapses inside and applies pressure to the wounded knee. Sirens wail down the main road as several campers shuffle in their tents, stepping out to view what crisis unfolds at their campsite. With ambulances and firetrucks racing down the road, adult campers start rumors, and they quickly make their way through the area. His heart pounding, the boy struggles to regain his normal breathing in his tent, appearing asleep through it all. Sirens fade into the distance and are not heard again that night.

***

The following Monday arrives after an eventful weekend at the lake. Consumed with nagging curiosity, the boy swipes a sandwich from a distracted student's tray and bolts through a side door in the cafeteria. Shoving the turkey and cheese sandwich into his mouth, he pounds his feet into the broken concrete sidewalk and heads towards the local library.

Prying the two large doors apart, he walks inside and is caught off guard by a familiar face who recognizes him. "Hey there!" She smiles as she carries a stack of books to the back room. The girl, a gorgeous dirty blonde with a modern feathered haircut, is only a grade below him and seems to be helping around the place. Studying the girl from a distance, the boy recognizes her, but can't remember her name. The girl is a cheerleader at their middle school and comes from a broken home. She is quite popular and friendly to everyone she meets, never judging one person over another.

Checking out a solo book this time, the boy lays his selection of rattlesnakes down on the wooden counter. The young girl comes out from the back stock room and greets him with her southern Texas twang, "You remember me, right?" She writes down his book choice in the inventory log.

Shyly, he responds, "I remember your face, but I am not good with names, unfortunately."

She slides the form across the counter to him. Nervously, he accepts it.

"It's Grace—Gracie Williams from our school. I help here on the weekends, but they needed me today during my lunch break. You know, just help organize while everyone goes to lunch fast. I don't mind, really. I am saving as much money as I can so I can move out when I graduate."

Signing his name on the paper, he slides it back to her. "That's five years from now through?"

Looking down at his book, she places it in the paper sack and replies, "I know, but I don't have any family really, and I must rely on myself, you know? Sometimes it's just that way, and all you can do is be the best you can be."

Amazed by her maturity, the boy finds an instant attraction to her. "Can I ask what happened to the lady who worked here?"

A somber expression falls over her face. "It's the strangest thing. You're checking out a book on rattlesnakes, and Ms. Vicky died this past weekend at the lake from a Timber Rattlesnake bite. I just can't imagine. I've never seen those because we never go hiking or camping… But she was so sweet to me. So honestly, I am glad that you are researching this. You just never know, you know?"

Struggling between two different emotions, being proud of his fatal accomplishment and butterflies over the budding friendship, he nods in acceptance to her statement and simply smiles as he takes the paper sack in his hands. Feeling his cheeks growing hot, he turns his head down as he begins to blush. Not saying anything more, he heads to the double doors as a young Grace sweetly says, "See you later, Bobby Robinson."

The drive away from the old library feels longer than usual; the summer air is thick with the promise of change. Bobby tries to steady his nerves as he rounds the bend toward home, glancing at the paper sack resting on the passenger seat. Grace's words echo in his mind: "You just never know, you know?" He wonders if anyone ever really does. The rattlesnake book seems heavier now, weighted with new meaning. He thinks of Ms. Vicky, whose kindness touched so many except him, and how thin the line is between everyday life and tragedy.

As Bobby reaches his family's porch, the sun is already dipping behind the pecan trees. He pauses before going inside, catching his reflection in the dusty window. For the first time, he questions the path that has led him here, from nervous schoolboy to someone caught in a web of secrets. He resolves that tomorrow he will return to the library—maybe to see Grace, maybe just to find answers in the stacks. Until then, he'll try to carry the burden of both pride and guilt as best he can.

# Chapter 14

Present day

A sullen Bob Robinson, alongside his wife, Grace, makes their way back to the family cabin in the woods of Texas. Engrossed with grief and shock over everything that has happened, they realize they want to figure out a way to be closer to their son in some way. Due to the graphic nature of his decaying body, which decomposed so badly in the basement, the family makes the imperative decision to bury Ryan on site. They choose a covered area underneath a giant walnut tree that is easily seen from the kitchen window resting over the sink.

Grace and her mother-in-law had spent countless hours over the years in the kitchen preparing meals together and sharing new recipes with a young Ryan. There is no way to count the memories that were made. The cabin has always been their sanctuary, and they want to keep it that way.

This same year, four months after Ryan's death, his grandfather suddenly passed away in the nursing home. It is a devastating time for the family. His grandfather was placed in hospice through a mediocre company that the facility recommended. The family later wrote a letter to the director of the nursing home, saying they would never use their services again, detailing their almost unbearable experience. With that, Bob and Grace make the executive decision to move his mother, Mary, with them.

"Mary, would you like us to make you some hot tea with honey?" Grace politely asks.

"No, dear, what I have here is delightful," she responds. Mary looks down at her ketchup packets and vanilla cream cookies and begins preparing her latest concoction—cookies topped with ketchup. Gazing in her direction over the top of his newspaper from afar, Bob leaves his recliner and walks away as he gags. "Is this what you're going to do to me one day?" He barks at his wife.

Without missing a beat, she retorts, "She's your mother. Do not forget the apple never falls far from the tree."

Looking over some painting samples, Grace decides on a dark forest green for the exterior of the cabin as Bob pounds another shot of scotch in the corner of the living room. Grace, accepting things for what they are, makes her own plans and chooses to preserve the natural feel of the woods. Anything too bright or outlandish would be a disgrace to the land. After much deliberation, Grace ultimately persuades Bob to renovate the tiny wooden home into a retreat.

Mary's health declines, and her dementia diagnosis begins to overpower her brain. For the most part, she can still formulate full sentences; however, everyday tasks are quite a challenge. Completely incontinent, Mary wets herself and is at the point where using a wheelchair for risk of falling is necessary. The cabin is a single-story apart from the front deck steps and the basement. The steps to the deck are an easy fix as Grace orders a metal ramp online and has Bob install it. Mary simply wants to be near her only child… her son. At this point in her life, Grace completely understands.

***

At Renee's memorial site, which only holds childhood photos and stuffed animals, Grace decides to finally swallow her pride and deliver a handwritten letter after the murders. She recants her statement to the press on her daughter-in-law and chooses to part ways with her memory of her. Renee's parents passed away tragically in a car accident when she was only four years old, leaving her in the care of her grandmother, who also died unexpectedly while Renee was in her second year of college. No other family members existed to Renee that anyone was aware of.

The body of the beautiful red-haired Renee has never been found, so the Robinson family graciously donated a memorial site in a small, reserved park in her name. Each holiday, Grace lays out a delicate set of fresh flowers from the local florist. Orange always seemed to complement Renee's striking red curls, so Grace usually lays out stunning orange blooms, which contrast so brilliantly against her obsidian headstone.

The Robinsons continue their renovations over the summer and are finally complete as fall sets in at the cabin. For easy access, the lengthy gravel driveway is now a stunning black velvet sheet of freshly poured asphalt. The aroma of the new driveway beckons a proud Bob to race his mom up and down the driveway in her expensive wheelchair. She does not obey. From the outside, the cabin's fresh makeover easily welcomes the grieving family to a clean slate. The front door hinges are replaced. A new polyurethane sealant is applied throughout the applicable wood surfaces in the cabin. The cabin is tested for termites and successfully passes, saving the family thousands of dollars. Cabinets in the kitchen are gutted and replaced with a modern forest green, paired with elaborate gold hardware, complementing the modern trends of rural Texas. The counters and islands no longer wear vintage Formica; instead, they feature stunning black-and-white granite. The floors are refinished by a passionate company founded in Waco. A fresh coat of paint is applied where applicable. Most of the interior features original brick or woodwork, which are kept natural to preserve the vintage cabin's overall feel.

Grace would casually show up as the renovations unfolded, to rebuild a fresh start on her journey towards a brighter future. As days turn into weeks, she feels the welcoming presence of a home that also wants a fresh start. Upon removal of the old decor and replacing it with gold and warm tones, the cabin begins to take on a glamorous vibe.

Bob's father, who hand-carved a gun case in the 1960s, stands in the corner of the quaint living area, reminding Bob that he still cannot shoot a gun as well as his wife can. It is a popular topic of conversation that the reigning man of the home often avoids. Inside, it holds several rifles that are rarely handled. Bob could not tell one from the other.

Mary perches in her wheelchair in the dining room as she peers out the window into the woods. To the left is a well, the driveway, and Ryan's headstone. Behind the headstone, the pitch-black woods. Mary stares into the darkness for what seems like hours, not budging an inch. The sun completely falls from the horizon, signaling it is time for bed.

Grace arrives from behind and places her hands on Mary's shoulders. "Mom, are you getting tired?"

"There is something out there. There is something just beyond those trees. Don't you see it, Grace? He is so tall and majestic." She lifts her weathered hands and points directly towards Ryan's grave.

Peering out into the darkening forest, Grace sees a large shadow retreat out of sight and questions her vision.

Her stomach grows hard as she grasps the wheelchair's handles and drives it in reverse. "Momma, I did not see anything, but it may have been a deer or a small animal. Let us get you ready for bed."

The duo makes their way down to Ryan's old room, and Grace opens the door. The room is now fit-to-be-tied for an elderly woman. A vintage curio cabinet filled with pink, collectable Miss America Hocking dinnerware gleams against the glass and custom lighting. Grace had made the trip down to Houston months prior to retrieving the rare set of glassware. She gifted her mother-in-law the set as a welcome present for her old yet new home, now run by her son and daughter-in-law.

The bedding in Mary's room features a timeless pink-and-white floral pattern with a white lace trim. The bed frame is a 1960s vintage brass piece, thrifted by Grace herself. In the far corner of the room sits a historic pedestal table, complete with a 1900s wash basin and pitcher, lovingly placed atop a crocheted doily. Beside the doorway sits a family heirloom chair with a brunette porcelain doll in a white frilly dress. To complete the room, a set of drapes adorns the only window, matching the pattern of the bed set.

"Oh my… this feels just like a doll's house. I am over the moon!" Mary, cheers.

Changing her mother-in-law, Grace tucks the bedding around the small, framed woman and turns down the blinds to the window. "No! Do not fucking close those blinds, you dirty whore! And don't pull the drapes either!" Mary shouts.

Jumping back, Grace recoils her hands from the blinds as if they are hot coals. Startled, Grace mutters, "I'm sorry! I d-don't mean to upset you…"

Mary stares straight into the window, arching her neck and looking back. As Grace unsteadily backs into the doorway, Mary replies, "I want to be able to see outside when Ryan's friend comes to visit me." Sharply cocking her head back to Grace, Mary commands, "Now get the fuck out, BITCH."

Grace's jaw falls wide open in shock. Without a word, she sits down at the dining room table for the rest of the night and stares out the window toward the forest. The moonlight glows as the tree limbs sway between it and the house. *"Did I severely confuse my mother-in-law, or is something far worse transpiring?"* She thinks to herself. It takes everything she has to forget the details of Ryan's gruesome death, but now the memories are trying to force themselves back into her life. Thoughts uncontrollably race without permission through her brain, one right after the next.

*"Who is she talking about? She's crazy. She must be. There's nobody within miles of here. The police did a flight overhead and scanned the entire property. The cadaver dogs smelled nothing for*

*miles. It's absurd. She's hallucinating. I'm not telling Bob about this because it's ridiculous."*

Grace pops a melatonin in her mouth and takes a big gulp of water to wash it down. She chooses to sleep on the couch for the rest of the night and falls asleep within minutes, dreaming of a deep, dark hole in the ground filled with bones and weathered skin. A vision that leaves an indelible mark on her mind.

# Chapter 15

Grace awakens to the sound of her husband making scrambled eggs in the kitchen. The mouthwatering smell of bacon infiltrates the air of the cabin, making it feel like a small diner tucked away at a resort.

"Long night?" Bob looks over at a groggy Grace. She nods gently and eases her way into the kitchen to pour herself a cup of black coffee. "I'm going out to the bar with the guys tonight. It's pool night, and they want to catch up on things. You know, since I don't need to be here all the damn time," Bob states without question.

Grace remembers what her mother-in-law said the night before and brushes it off, believing that it is some fantasy she dreamt up or just sundowner's syndrome. Looking down, she defeatedly replies, "Okay. If you need a ride, call one. I don't want you to wreck the truck. Where is your mom?" she questions.

"Oh, she's outside. Exactly right over there." Bob points a spatula toward the edge of the driveway through the window. "I couldn't tell her otherwise. Damn old lady. She was fucking rude this morning."

Looking over her shoulder and out the dining room window, Grace lays eyes on a white-haired Mary, sitting in her wheelchair next to Ryan's headstone, facing the edge of the woods. "What on earth…" Grace says under her breath, pushing herself up from the table. "With her attitude this morning, who cares what she does?" Bob laughs.

Grace hastily slides on her sandals and runs through the driveway towards the edge of the woods to retrieve her mother-in-law. Pine needles poke her toes as she runs. Standing above the eighty-nine-year-old woman, who hardly has on a nightgown, Grace carefully starts, "Mom? Mom, what are you doing all the way out here?" Grace turns to face the trance-like state that had overcome Mary and pleads, "Mary! Can you please say something to me? Are you okay? Why are you all the way out here?"

Slowly turning her pale, caked face to her side, and then steadily upward to make eye contact with her daughter-in-law, Mary cracks open a wide grin and calmly states, "Did you know that they rotted, dear?"

Taken aback, Grace stutters, "Wh… what?"

"It's true! They rotted under the floorboards. They rotted in the hole, and they will continue to rot until it gets hold of what it wants."

Mary raises her shoulders in a cute little gesture and lets out a mocking giggle. Turning to face the woods again, she softly says, "Oh, I am so excited. He's coming."

A cold, shrill shudder runs throughout Grace's body as she suddenly questions her own psychological state.

The day continues as if nothing happened. Once again, Grace chalks up the conversation from earlier to nothing more than a bad spell of dementia. She has several nurse friends back home who specialize in memory care, and some of the stories they share at parties are more than unsettling. Some are so comical that they *wanted* to share. One of her best friends, Shandi, plans to author a small book on the quotes and stories that have happened over her nursing career. Grace agrees it is worth taking a shot at.

Grace picks a fun movie for a girl's night with Mary, alongside stovetop popcorn and a bottle of merlot. The wine is for Grace; she needs it.

Bob sets off for the evening to Merle, where his gang of friends always meet, without saying goodbye to his wife. Grace watches through the curtain as he drives away in the truck; the heavy scent of cologne lingers throughout the cabin. Accepting it for what it is, Grace knows he doesn't even wear cologne on their dates together, which are far and few between. Her heart aches in pain.

The bar— not too packed, yet never boring or slow—is the central location for each of the men, enabling the young, flirtatious staff to cater to their needs. The grown group of men eats it up. The servers are voluptuous, makeup-perfected, and eager to be stared at by men twice their age. The bar shut down at 2 AM, with last call at one-thirty AM.

About a quarter of the way through the film, Grace feels a dreadful pain in her gut as the night draws on. The air fills with a mouth-watering buttery popcorn aroma that Mary can't get enough of. Occasionally, a popcorn kernel gets stuck in her dentures, and Grace helps remove it.

With the breeze of autumn wafting into the central part of Texas, Grace decides it is a wonderful time to air out the cabin, so she opens each window, sending the lightweight ivory curtains fluttering like delicate swans. It's the most serene vibe, setting the tone for a relaxing evening.

Rounding out the night, Grace lets Mary stay in Bob's oversized recliner, which sits directly in front of the television set. Mary was calm and sweet the entire night, making Grace wish her mother-in-law could stay that way.

The empty bottle of merlot sits on the coffee table as the local TV station plays reruns of vintage black-and-white shows, forcing the two women to ease into the midnight hour as the heavy weight of sleep overtakes them.

# The Hollow

Grace awakens a few hours later, drenched in sweat. She sits up straight on the couch and peers around the room to regain her bearings. Realizing she had passed out cold, she looks at the empty wine bottle on the coffee table. The once-entertaining show has turned into a grey and white haze on the television. She suddenly feels as if she had been thrust back in time. Grace feels a sense of relief as Mary lies undisturbed in the recliner, all thanks to her nightly medications. It's after 2 AM, and Bob's small terrain truck isn't in the front driveway. Grace looks at her cell phone, showing no recent text messages. The service isn't the best, as few internet providers serve this part of Texas. The area is extremely desolate.

She decides to shut off the small television and lights a large apple-scented candle on the dining room table, sensing Bob would show up any minute. Sifting through some old photo albums on the fluffy rug beneath her, she reminisces over decades' worth of pictures. The memories caress her heart as she turns page by page, some yellowing from years of cigarette smoke. There is a slight moldy smell to the albums, since they had been kept in the cabin for the entirety of their lives. To Grace, they are simply perfect. The scent drifts into her senses as she remembers her own grandparents and the way that their home smelled: brown shag carpets and wood paneled walls, swag lights conveniently hanging over pedestal ashtrays at the end of every couch and chair. They all spark a memory for her, and it starts with the smell of the old photo album. Innocence and security. Corded phone calls in each room and home-cooked meals for days. Grace wishes she could go back in time.

Grace checks on a snoring Mary and walks to the bathroom down the narrow hallway. She decides to take a quick shower and gets herself ready for another night on the couch. Rinsing off under the hot water, she turns off the faucet and wraps a large, tattered towel around her. The air is so thick with steam that she must open the hallway door to air out the tiny space. Looking down at her phone, she feels sick to her stomach. Not a single message from Bob. She wraps her dripping blonde hair in a smaller towel and quietly tiptoes down the hall to check on Mary in the main room. Leaning subtly beyond the end corner of the hallway, she notices a plume of white hair peaking over the back of the recliner, as it casually rocks forward, then backward, forward, then backward. The cabin grows eerily quiet as the curtains continue to float in the cool air. The room feels darker even with the large burning candle on the dining room table. Grace clutches the top of her towel, keeping it wrapped around her body.

Slowly making her way around the recliner, Grace hears the steady ticking of the grandfather clock in the black corner of the living room, opposite the television set. Holding her breath, she rounds the recliner and stops dead in her tracks. Looking down, she slows her gaze upon a wide-eyed, grinning Mary, her eyes pitch-black, staring straight ahead at a picture on the wall above the television. Grace slowly turns her head as she lays eyes on a small-framed picture from decades before. Before her is a small boy, centered, with cold, heartless eyes glaring straight into the camera. Dating back to the mid-1960s, a young Bob Robinson angrily stares through the dusty glass frame.

Mary continues to rock herself as the gentle creaking of the recliner echoes against the ticking clock. The entire scene sends shivers through Grace, who begins to tremble, an unsettling feeling overwhelming her. She struggles to catch her breath. Her words are trapped inside, unable to escape. She desperately wants to hear a truck pull into the driveway to save her, but that does not happen.

The recliner stops rocking, and the clock goes silent. The air in the cabin plummets to freezing cold as Grace watches her breath suddenly form in the air.

*"POP, POP! CRAAACKKKK!!"* The sounds of breaking limbs and falling trees come through the open windows.

Tears flow down Grace's cheeks as she cowers into a nearby wall. Horrible sounds escalate from outside as heavy footsteps make their way around the outside perimeter of the cabin, as if circling it. With every step, crunching sounds soon fall behind.

*"CRUNCH, CRUUNCH, CRUUNNCHH!"*

Grace is trembling so badly at this point that a well of vomit surges from her chest. Wine mixed with stomach acid spews from her mouth and nostrils, igniting a painful burning, causing her to cough and cry at the same time. Taking her towel from her upper body, she removes it and covers her saturated face to remove the acid. She blows her nose into the towel and raises her eyes. Mary slowly turns her head into the darkness and stares directly at Grace, her eyes filled with an empty black nothingness.

"The words are hidden in the hole. They're hidden below, where no one can find them." Mary cackles with laughter and starts up again. "Ole' Cooper got what he deserved, didn't he? He tasted quite nice. Why don't you go into the hole, dearie? You might learn a thing or two about that son of yours. We're so proud of him down here." Mary smiles proudly and rejoices in a language that Grace has never heard before. 'Oh, doladie oh doladie, thrumbstock weee doeeeee! Fosch emi yeh tooo zouhhhh!" She suddenly stops and holds up her right hand to her ear, as if to listen to something from afar. *"Crack, crack!! Oh, I feel a break! How about a good thrust! Slam it in! STRETCCHHHH!!!!!"*

And with that, Mary belts out in horrific laughter, forcing the entire cabin to convulse. Pictures fall from shelves as glass shatters on the floor. Rugs rotate from their original positions underneath small tables and chairs. The entire site is too much. Burying herself on the floor at the end of the hallway, Grace aggressively cups her ears to drown out the satanic laughter. It echoes so violently that Grace's cries for peace could not be heard. Shivering from the cold, she suddenly feels warmth overcome her when, out of nowhere, an inebriated Bob grasps her hands and shakes her with fury.

"What the fuck is going on, Grace?" Bob demands, spewing fumes in her face.

She pulls back aggressively through the tears and fires back at him. "Where have you been? It's well after the bar closes, and I'm scared! Something isn't right in this cabin, Bob! Something evil is in here, and it's affecting your mom and me!"

Laughingly, he fumbles back into the wall and belligerently retorts, "You're a fucking crazy-ass bitch. Listen to yourself. I'm going to bed! Get your shit together and take your meds before you get put in a fucking psych hospital."

Looking downward, he aggressively spits on her bare feet and walks away, slamming the master bedroom door. Without hesitation, he bolts it shut from the inside, locking her out.

Sobbing, Grace angrily gets herself up from the floor, realizing this is on her to fight. She forces herself into the main room, lifts her mother-in-law, and puts her to bed. Mary innocently stares at Grace, watching her every move, as if she were put in time out for stealing a classmate's toy. She steps out into the main room, pacing the floor. She checks closets and bathrooms. She gives Mary another dose of melatonin, saying, *"This is for you, please take it."*

Mary takes the pill given to her, and it lasts no more than a few minutes before her eyes close, and a deep slumber takes over. This time, the blinds and curtains are tightly shut. No questions are allowed.

Anger and frustration control every aspect of Grace's body. She slams every window shut in the home while reciting her favorite prayers to herself. Recalling what Mary had said moments earlier, she retrieves an old notebook and pen from the kitchen and thinks, "Something about her son. Something about a hole."

Taking the pen into her right hand, she closes her eyes. Drowning out the ticking of the clock, she travels back in her memory to retrieve what Mary had said.

She begins to write. "The words are hidden in the hole. They're hidden below, where no one can find them."

Staring over the script, her head feels as if it could explode from a night's worth of pressure and trauma. She lies back on the couch and, without realizing, falls into a deep sleep. The notebook and pen slide onto the floor, closing the pages shut.

# Chapter 16

The next morning, Grace awakens to find an empty home. She walks into the kitchen, her feet not functional, and reads a note Bob left her on the counter.

*"I'm taking mom out this morning for breakfast in Merle, then shopping in Waco since she's clearly too much for you to handle... - Bob."*

Grace sighs in relief. The drive from Merle to Waco is about two hours, so they would be gone most of the day. Mary would sleep on the way there and the way back.

Grace finds a key lime Greek yogurt in the fridge with some fresh strawberries and decides to have a light breakfast on the front deck with her black coffee. It is a morning that she desperately needs, and Bob isn't taking things seriously. Grace tries to relax as she focuses on a more positive mindset. The trees, the cool fall breeze. It is quite easy to get lost in the natural beauty of the woods. Not a single person walking past the house, and no sounds of traffic or blaring horns. Just complete peace. For the most part, anyway.

Regardless of how hard Grace tries to focus, her mind continues to wander off. She quickly rises from her seat and retrieves the notebook from the night before. Returning to her chair on the deck, she takes a sip of hot coffee and stares at the words.

"Hole."

"What is she talking about exactly?" Grace thinks to herself. "Surely, she isn't talking about Ryan's grave? Because that is not happening." She shudders at the thought of exhuming her son's remains. "Wait. RYAN. Oh, my goodness, the basement!" she exclaims to herself.

Grabbing her things from the small table, Grace rushes inside. Standing in front of the basement door, she draws a deep breath. She hasn't been down there yet. A small wave of anxiety floods over her. Without giving it a second more, she unlocks the door and gently pulls it open to reveal a narrow set of dark, wooden stairs leading to a pit of secrets. To the left is the old flashlight—the exact one that her son used when he died. Somehow, it miraculously stayed in the cabin. She holds it in the daylight of the hallway, noticing the traces of deep red still embedded in the grooves of the handle. Tears well up inside her.

Pushing them down, she turns on the light and descends into the murky darkness.

Reaching the foot of the wooden stairs, she shines the light in a steady sweeping motion from left to right. Feeling her chest begin to tighten, she takes a deep breath and looks upward, saying a short prayer to herself. After a few moments, she starts with the left side of the room, the side where Ryan was discovered. Throughout the room, there is truly little as far as items or furniture are concerned. A couple of old wooden chairs, lanterns that probably don't work… nothing out of the ordinary. The original rock wall that encompasses the room is the only thing that stands out.

Thinking back, she focuses on the words. *"The words are hidden in the hole. They're hidden below, where no one can find them."*

"There must be something down here. A letter, a note, a carving… something must be down here," she says to herself. With that, she decides to start from one end of the rock wall as she shines the light on every possible nook and cranny. She makes her way around the room as she comes to the last part of the wall. Not seeing anything, she grows increasingly frustrated and loses hope.

Sitting at the bottom of the stairs, she lets out a stressful sigh and buries her face in her hands. Tears wet her palms as she realizes she is fighting a bigger battle. Pulling her old T-shirt over her face to dry her eyes, she reaches to pick up the light as something catches her eye from underneath the bottom step.

"Oh, my God," she says.

Underneath the bottom wooden step, a dusty journal is securely fastened by two leather straps and four small screws. The journal easily slides in and out for easy access. No one can see it unless they are looking at the ground. It is incredible.

Grace takes the small book out of its cradle and at once leaves the basement in relief. In desperate need of fresh air, she returns to her post on the front deck. In her own privacy, she leafs through the hidden token as if it is an ancient piece of history that has just been discovered.

The dates inside indicate it to be from his seventh-grade year. Thinking back, she remembers that was the last time they came to visit before Bob's parents went into the nursing home. The family didn't see much of Ryan that holiday because he…

She pauses, her eyes growing wide. Lifting her head from the book, she stares across the way at Ryan's headstone. She quickly remembers how he constantly went into the woods, almost every single day for hours at a time.

Looking back down at the journal, she sifts through the book, holding each sheet delicately between her fingers. Detailed drawings of pure horror lay on aged sheets of dirty, damp paper. Only a quarter of the way through, Grace turns the page to something even darker.

Not understanding what she is looking at, she reaches for her phone and goes straight to the internet. Searching for anything that resembles the small dictations, she sets the book down on the small table and rests her elbows on her knees, leaning over to concentrate on her search. After several minutes, she finally lands on an exact match. Tapping the icon with her right index finger takes her to a website. The website prompts her to agree that she is eighteen or older.

Hesitant to acknowledge, she stops and feels a dreadful reaction in her gut. The website is completely black, with the prompt in a maroon font throughout. There is a small symbol that matches what is on Ryan's journal entry.

Realizing she needs to know her son to understand better what is going on in the cabin, she draws in a sharp breath and slowly pushes it out.

Curiosity wins her over. She presses the consent box.

# Chapter 17

Staring at the screen of her phone, Grace wishes she could forget her past and simply feel safe and happy.

The gut-wrenching sickness impales her as she slowly scrolls through the disturbing images that match perfectly to her son's diagrams. Before her are impeccably drawn images reflecting a satanic language.

Shuffling through the journal, her mind at once realizes how sick Ryan had really been, and what's worse, he had brought an evil entity into their home. She is scared and feels a wave of guilt for never truly knowing her son.

*"Why didn't he reach out? I did my best to support him and arranged therapy, so he'd have someone impartial to talk to. I wanted*

*him to have someone that he could confide in, who he felt safe with. I wasn't enough for him."*

Tears stream down Grace's cheeks as she feels her heart breaking. The pain invades her shoulders and soars behind her ears. Setting her phone between her feet on the deck, she breaks down and decompresses her aching spirit, accepting that she would have never fully known his truth.

*"What thirteen-year-old child produces these kinds of ideas? Why would he willingly pursue something he knows is so wrong? He was brought up better than that. We would have never encouraged him toward Satan. He was just sick, sick in his mind."* She goes through each thought as her tears fall onto her phone.

At that moment in time, she thinks of Renee. Her heart aches for her as she paints a demented picture of what her daughter-in-law had unknowingly been living with. The amount of deception she went through. "I am truly sorry," Grace whispers. Closing out the website and the journal, she vows never to reopen the journal.

The time is now 11:45 AM. Grace enters the cabin and stops dead in her tracks. An epiphany shoots through her like a dagger, piquing her interest. Not only had there been an evil force battling against Ryan, but he had also welcomed it into the cabin years earlier. "Oh, dear Jesus," Grace exclaims.

Fearing the worst, yet realizing the more she knows, the better, she pulls on a pair of worn walking shoes and heads for the front door.

Taking a step back, she turns to her right and reaches the entryway shelf to grab Bob's dusty switchblade. She tucks the blade into her sports bra and heads straight for the woods, without thinking of grabbing anything else. She takes note of the time on her watch and vacates the cabin.

Fixating on the direction that Mary is so obsessed with, Grace enters the dense woods, passing right by Ryan's grave. Already stepping into two potholes, she quickly realizes they are easily hidden underneath decades' worth of brush and debris. Avoiding making a step too abrupt, Grace struggles not to turn an ankle or impale herself on a sharp limb. Of all places, if she is to go missing, no one would think of looking for her in the woods. Being more of a city girl, she almost never went hiking.

To secure her balance, she seeks a strong walking stick from the ground and continues into the deepest part of the forest. The time is almost 1 PM. She needs to figure something out before Bob and Mary return, or at least before the sun goes down.

As she progresses further, a small clearing with tall grass presents before her eyes. The lack of birds and small animals heightens her senses as she studies the area. Walking approximately twenty feet in front of her, she unknowingly enters the medial part of the woods and plummets first into a deep hollow hole, her wrists catching her fall. A shrill of pain wails from Grace as she lies weakly in the sunken hole. Regaining her bearings after a few minutes, she props herself against the damp wall of dirt and closes her eyes, decompressing her emotions. Slowly turning her head left and right with her eyes closed, she sorts through her memory of Ryan's journal entries. Opening her eyes, she steadies her head and focuses on an object in front of her. Leaning closer, Grace raises her right hand and gently touches the end of what seems to be struggling for a way out from the feet of dirt. Sensing a dark secret unfolding in front of her, Grace wraps her fingers around the object and pulls it towards her. Dirt falls around her feet as more white shards become clear in the wall.

Horrified, Grace lets out a desperate scream filled with panic. She viciously shakes as she struggles to kick the object off her. Not only is it a large bone, but it is a femur that clearly belonged to a human corpse.

Throwing herself backwards from the mound, she swiftly retracts her hands inward, hugging her chest in a dire need for security. She has never seen a bone this large before, and she most certainly has never touched one. Realizing she must push herself further, she collects her walking stick and digs at the wall, exposing a more diabolical scheme. The unsightly contents unfold before her as she becomes aware that a mixture of both humans and animals is buried in the grave. Turning herself in a full circle, she prepares herself for more bones to present themselves through the burial site. Shoving her walking stick throughout each wall of the hole, she finds tufts of hair and various shards of skull, bone, and fur caked in soil.

Gazing closer to a section on the left, she notices small, handwritten letters attached to some of the bones and recognizes the writing almost at once. Only a few hours prior, she held similar writings in her hands. Grace has seen enough. Prying her bruised and aching body out of the hole, she races back to the cabin in a desperate effort to distance herself from the pit of hell.

# Chapter 18

Rinsing off in a steaming hot shower before Bob and Mary return from a day in Waco, Grace processes the events of her day so rapidly in her mind that her head aches. In a slight state of shock, she exits the shower and takes a healthy dose of pain medication to cure her physical ailments.

Grace double-checks the bolt on the front door and the locks on all the windows. She looks at her phone to see that it is 4:45 PM. She decides to lie down on the couch to rest before Bob and Mary return. Within a matter of minutes, she is fast asleep; her medicine works accordingly.

****

An hour later, Grace wakes up to the truck doors shutting out front. They have finally returned. Opening the front door, she notices the sun is still out, sending a reassuring wave of comfort through her. For the first time in her adult life, she realizes she is afraid of the dark. A red-faced Bob wheels a tiresome Mary up the ramp. Grace notices several brand-name bags in her lap, showing a day's worth of expensive shopping. Rounding the corner, Bob glances over at the small journal on the table with a curious look. The smell of alcohol sears Grace's nostrils. He is on the verge of being completely drunk. Trying to brush it off, Grace hastily picks up the old journal and says, "From when I was a kid," and smiles at him, knowing he will never be interested in it.

Inside, a blissful Mary tells of the small trip and everything they ate. Standing in Mary's bedroom doorway, Grace lovingly admires how adorable Mary is in her petite wheelchair as she excitedly lays out her new possessions on her pink and white floral bed set. Grace has never seen her happier, and it reminds her of when she herself was a little kid at Christmas time, doing the exact thing with her beloved gifts.

Small, little trinkets of this and that sparkle in the sunset as the hand-painted faces of porcelain dolls smile back at her. In total, Mary now has six of them, almost making Grace unsure of Mary's décor choice. Aside from the creepy dolls, she clearly had a momentous day venturing from one antique shop to the next, finding wonderful pieces to add to her new room. It is a sight that warms Grace's heart and instills a sense of hope.

Bob goes straight to the refrigerator and cracks open a beer. Unsure of what to say to her husband, Grace chooses to stay by Mary's side, feeling it is the safest choice.

"Are you good for the night?" Bob questions as he gives his wife a judgmental look. Grace already knows what he is getting at.

As the cool, autumn night sets in, a loud, *"CRACK!"* sounds abruptly from outside the dining room window, causing Bob to jolt from his stupor on the kitchen island. Looking over to the curtained window, he snarls, "What the hell! Dumbass wind."

Grace's chest fills with immense dread as she watches her belligerent husband in solace. Grabbing his keys and wallet, Bob laughs to himself in a pitiful attempt to act tough. Walking straight past his wife, he opens the door to the cabin and makes his way out, slamming the wooden door behind him. Grace stands up abruptly from the couch and runs to the front porch in a desperate attempt to reach his attention. Not giving a second glance at where his wife is standing, Bob starts up the only vehicle the couple has at the cabin and disappears through the weaving driveway of tall trees.

***

Alone with a sleeping Mary, the grandfather clock chimes eleven times. Taking in each chime, Grace clutches her bible as she stares out the window into the nothingness that exists under the moonlight of the swaying trees. The cabin is dark and almost too quiet for comfort. Turning to the refrigerator, she decides to open a bottle of wine and pour a tall glass to ease her nerves. Sucking down the first few swallows, she doesn't hesitate to let the fermented beverage breathe. The events of Grace's day are enough to wreck anyone, mentally and physically.

Picking up Ryan's journal, she places it in a large metal bucket under the sink and takes it to the front deck with a box of matches. She gently sets her glass on the little table and strikes a match, understanding that what she is about to do can never be reversed. This journal had to be one of Ryan's most prized possessions, as it was so important to him that he felt the need to keep its secrecy hidden away. Now knowing the depths of his reasoning for concealing it for all those years, endless pages of depraved and diabolical information did not sway Grace's determination.

Recalling the horror she had read and seen earlier in the day, she willingly lets go of the lit match and sets the journal on fire.

A symbolic burst of elaborate flames glows fiercely against the metal sheen. Relief lifts her heart and carries her broken spirit into the air, as white clouds of smoke dance in the night sky. Each burning page curls elegantly and transforms into black ash as the heat moves toward the book's center, consuming its dark, twisted contents.

Sitting down on the same chair she had sat on hours before, Grace tosses back the glass of merlot and retrieves another filled glass from inside. Hearing only pure silence, she makes her way back to the front deck, securing a sleeping Mary. She clearly had an amazing day with her son, and that is enough for Grace. She takes another taste of her dark, red wine and leans back in her chair, watching the flames commence before her. Peering toward her son's grave, she catches a glimpse of a tall, dark figure darting through the moonlight on the edge of the tree line just beyond the headstone. She shoots up from her chair as she feels her heart hardening with fear. It bolts so fast that there is no way it is human.

Striving to move, she forces herself back into the dark cabin and bolts the wooden door. Paralyzed with fear, Grace, holding her breath, turns toward the dining room window. Under the light of the moon, an enormous shadow is cast down against the moonlight. A steady rhythm of crunching leaves pounds into the ground, casting eerie shadows throughout each window. Listening to the heavy footsteps around the perimeter of the cabin, Grace feels the pressure in her head escalating to a pounding headache. Her breathing hastens. Suddenly, the footsteps stop. Grace catches a glimpse of a small piece of white fabric swaying mid-air down the hallway. Leaning forward, she inches toward it as a pale-faced Mary stands upright in the middle of the hallway, her eyes pitch black and glaring right at her.

A demonic laughter breaks from her mouth. "Do you know what your son did! Your precious baby boy!" Wails of terror cause the house to crack in various places as tension mounts to a pinnacle of pure evil. Crying out, Mary exclaims, "Your son fucked those animals! YOU DUMB, STUPID BITCH. He fucked them while they were dead! *Crack! Crack! Oh, we feel a break!* Another thrust to give him the time of his life… separate its hollow torso. And YOU were SO proud of that impish fool— Teacher of the Year!"

Mary cackles her sadistic torment as Grace races to the gun cabinet and pulls out a rifle, only to find that it is not loaded. Charging at Grace with an unearthly force, the possessed Mary knocks the two women into the back wall as she stealthily wraps her hands around Grace's face and shoves her thumbs into her eyes. Roaring screams from Mary continue to shake the entire cabin as Grace's eyes and ears are pierced in pain.

Headlights shine through the front windows of the house. Mary stops and retreats to an unknown location in the cabin, and the home falls silent. Not a single noise is heard. Grace struggles onto her arms and knees as she tries to regain her balance and eyesight. Bob fumbles his keys, dropping them on the front porch as he tries to unlock the door. In a drunken state, he lets out a slew of curse words as the door unlocks itself. Stumbling into the dark cabin, Bob pauses for a moment, hearing only the eerie silence, seeing only his shadow on the floor against the light of the moon.

Cautiously, he takes two steps inside and peers further into the darkness, feeling unsteady. He finally hears Grace whimper in the corner of the living room, but ignores her. She yells at him from the floor below. He loses his temper, and a flood of rage overtakes him as he grabs a fistful of dirty blonde hair and drags her to the moonlit entryway. Grabbing her by the throat with both hands, he slams her back into the hardened walls of the entryway. Bob slowly suffocates his petite wife as she struggles to catch a single gasp of air while her small fists violently fight back to save her life.

"You did this! You did this to my family! You fucked everything up and have been for years!" Bob screams. "This is MY house, and I want you out!" The stench of alcohol on his breath penetrates the air as Grace's vision turns dark. Suddenly, Bob feels a cool breeze shoot through the front door of the cabin, and an unearthly stench follows. Turning slowly toward the open doorway, Bob sees a dark, shadowy figure standing patiently and quietly on the front lawn. No longer interested in his dying bride, he casually lets go of her throat, hearing only a heavy drop to the floor below. Not looking in her direction once, Bob stares in wonderment, his mouth gaping open in veneration. Struggling to reclaim her breath, Grace gasps harshly for air as blood rushes back into her brain. Her vision slowly recovers as small objects here and there begin to take shape.

Folding itself in half to clear the doorway, the giant skeletal creature enters the cabin and fluidly crawls directly over her whimpering body, seemingly not the target of its visit. The creature slowly rises to its full frame against the moonlight. Bob arches his neck back to view the spectacle before him. In a pitiful attempt to escape the five-foot reach the monster has on him, Bob sobers up within seconds as panic sets in.

Creeping closer, it snatches Bob's collared polo, drags him effortlessly closer, and breathes in every ounce of fear as Bob begins to pour sweat. Coming within inches of the creature's darkened face, Bob feels a weight in his stomach turn as he becomes incredibly nauseated. Seizing the two-hundred-pound Bob, the creature hoists his body completely from the floor and into midair. Bones crack and pop as they shift. Bob smells every effluvium breath that hits his face, bringing on a viscous convulsion from the rotting smell. Yellow discharge erupts from the creature's snarling mouth as it pours all over the front of Bob's $200 luxury polo. Savoring every second, the colossal creature lets out an immeasurable roar, reverberating Bob's eardrums in a searing pain.

Feeling his right eardrum burst, he says, "I am sorry!! Please forgive me for what I have done. It wasn't me… it was—"

Failing to finish his sentence, frothy, hot beer mixed with stomach acid erupts violently from his stomach. Tears flow from the corners of his eyes. Not able to produce another word, acid burns through his esophagus and nostrils.

Bob realizes that every part of his duplicitous life since the spring of 1984 has owned him up to this very moment.

# Chapter 19

The creature takes his bony hands and effortlessly snaps the head of Bob Robinson in a split second. Bob's 200-pound body plummets to the floor, as a clanking sound of metal falls from Bob's left hand and bounces across the room into the dark. Grace sits straight up against the entryway wall, her respirations shallow and her eyes tired and bruised. Turning to face her, the tufts of hair move back and forth along the smooth, fall air as the bones of multiple animals kneel before her. Looking into the eyes of a gentle creature, her fear slowly melts away.

Unexpectedly, the creature straightens its complex body completely upright; its senses heightened. Alarmed, it cocks its head and crouches down into a defensive stance almost completely parallel to the wood floor. Grace feels a surge of fear as she stops breathing altogether so as to not distract the creature inches in front of her. The night temperature plunges to a freezing cold, as the creature and Grace's breath suddenly shoots out in steamy gusts from their mouths. Snarling with anger, the creature defensively creeps into the pitch-black hallway, its bones cracking and popping in pain from the icy climate.

Stopping in the middle of the hall, it turns its head to the left and runs its slender fingers through the door leading down into the basement.

"Oh, God, please don't…" Grace cries to herself in fear. The creature disappears into the basement.

Freezing to death from the plummeting temperatures, Grace forces herself over to the gun cabinet and pulls out a drawer from the bottom. Inside, there are several boxes of rounds, none of them resonating with her at this moment. Taking her fingers and forcefully pushing them into her right temple, she repeats, "Think, Grace! Think! You know this." Grasping the box at the back of the drawer, she remembers the boxes go with the guns in the case, starting left and ending right. Loading the gun as fast as she can, she picks herself up from the floor when a shining gleam catches her eye. Triggering something from within, she painfully kneels over the coffee table and retrieves the shining object in the moonlight, pocketing the small item.

Carefully, she rounds the corner of the living room, trying not to knock anything over, and faces the dark hallway. Not a sound is heard. She inches her way towards the open door of the basement and stops at the top of the stairs. Feeling her childhood trauma kick in, Grace instinctively racks the rifle and points it into the darkness. Feeling for the flashlight on the shelf to the left, she recognizes its shape and grasps the reliable piece with her left hand, thumbing the light on. Peering down the wooden steps, she shines the light only to see the first three steps before her. After all this time, the batteries begin to give out slowly, leaving her in a state of dire panic. The light shuts off completely as she is only on the first step.

Finding her faith and, reminding herself that, at this point, she has nothing to lose, Grace recites her favorite prayer from the Bible as she closes her eyes and listens. Over the course of two decades, she has countlessly made her way into the basement. Listening and feeling her surroundings, with her finger on the trigger, she slowly descends each step, hearing nothing except her own breathing and the creaking wood under her feet. With each step, her heart pounds even harder as her right hand nervously trembles and drips cold sweat from the grip of the gun.

Grace suddenly stops midway down the stairs. A gust of air blows from behind the step and hits the back of her ankles. The soft giggle of a little old woman sends Grace flying up the stairs, but a cold, hardened set of hands grabs her ankles. Grace pulls the trigger, sending a round into the ceiling above her. Debris covers the steps as the hands violently pull backwards, causing her to tumble down the stairs and onto the ground. Hitting her head against the rock wall, Grace feels a warm trickle of blood down her cheek, touching the corner of her mouth. Dizzy and concussed from her fall, she lies helplessly on the ground, losing the location of the rifle. A small, petite frame comes out from the shadows behind the stairs. Slowly raising herself enough to leverage her own weight, Grace pushes herself against the freezing rock wall, shivering with fear. Not having an ounce of energy left in her, she mumbles her prayer once more, in acceptance of what is about to come.

Mary steps closer as a small amount of light illuminates her face, showing solid black eyes and pointed teeth, hissing at her. Mary's white hair is wild and filthy. Her hands reach out in front of her, just as the unfolding and cracking of the massive creature appears directly behind her small frame. In an instant, Grace clutches the shiny object and shoves it into Mary's mouth, forcing her to swallow it whole. A shocked look sweeps over her face as she realizes what she just swallowed. Bob's silver coin that controlled his entire life now swims in the belly of the possessed mother-in-law. The creature takes its right hand and shoves it through Mary's spine, clenching her entire spinal cord, and ripping it out. It throws the cord against the wall behind them, so powerfully that it causes a loud smacking sound against the rocks.

Taking both its hands around her dirty white head, it twists it completely off, sending black blood all over Grace. Stooping to a lower level to come close to Grace's face, the creature looks directly into her eyes and gently wipes some of the blood from her face. A small tear rolls down her cheek as she feels a familiar feeling of deep affection well up inside of her. The evil is gone.

*** 

The creature's eyes… its beating heart… rises from the ground. The once-freezing temperatures restore back to normal. The tall figure carries the heavily bruised Grace up the stairs and gently sits her on the sofa. Stepping back—bones creaking—it pauses lovingly and heads back into the darkness of the night. Crawling her way over to the door, Grace leans out just enough to see the creature vanish into the woods beyond Ryan's grave. She lies her head down on the dirty wooden floor and sobs. Life, as she knows it, is completely over.

Grace lifts her head to see the small truck parked just around the corner from the side of the cabin. It is time. Reaching for her phone and purse from the dining area, she slowly makes her way through the room, relying on furniture to support her. Looking around the small home, she realizes nothing else in the cabin matters at this point. Everything feels tainted, and she has no one left. Gathering what little bit of courage she has, a completely drained Grace steps out onto the deck and retrieves the keys from a small nook on the porch where Bob had dropped them. Each bend of her body is almost too much to bear. Rising from the nook, something catches the corner of her eye.

Against the dark wood is a folded piece of paper at the edge of the steps. Next to it lie a small, handcrafted cross made from twigs and vines. Kneeling once more to retrieve the letter and small cross, Grace cautiously looks around before rising back up. There is nothing, and she hears nothing. Slowly unfolding the paper, she looks upon a scribbled message that is hard to make out.

Stepping out onto the asphalt driveway, she holds the paper toward the moon and is finally able to see what seems to be scratched out in dark charcoal.

In a familiar font that she recognizes. She reads the following message...

*"I'll always be here when you need me. I love you, Mom."*

Lifting her head at once towards Ryan's grave, she locks eyes with not one, but two figures. One is slightly taller and broader, and the other she knows as the one who saved her life. Across the way, they each blend perfectly into the night against the twigs and limbs that curve in complete disorder, showing the dense entrance to the miles of forest that now surrounds her like a security blanket. Grace gently nods in understanding and realizes everything that is happening. Her heart aches with memories of her little boy, knowing everything he had done ultimately led to this moment.

Her hands tremble as she stands under the moonlight, heart racing with a mix of dread and relief. The words on the paper, though simple, ignite a fragile hope inside her battered soul. Grace clutches the little cross tightly, pressing it to her chest as memories of Ryan's laughter echo faintly in her mind—a fleeting warmth amidst the darkness.

Taking a few steps towards the truck, she stops and looks back at the cabin, then back to the truck. Drawing in a deep breath, she holds the keys out in front of her and locks the truck. Two beeps sound, and she retracts her hand from the air. Staring up at the night sky, while taking in the fall breeze once more, she circles her body to soak up every inch of her son's woods. How beautiful they are, regardless of the secrets they hold. A sense of protection washes over her.

She is not alone. Feeling one last surge of energy, Grace goes up the wooden steps of the cabin to retrieve the bodies of her husband and mother-in-law. She pulls them to the front yard, knowing they will be gone by sunrise. "Getting them out of my cabin is the first step," she tells herself. She takes a hot bath with Epsom salts, opens a bottle of wine, and puts on one of Ryan's favorite jazz instrumental CDs. Finding her peace, she leaves the bloody messes on the floor for another day.

That night, for the first time in years, she sleeps with the door unlocked and the windows open. After months of investigation, nothing is produced but another unsolved missing person's case. Large imprints of mysterious feet deep in the woods, too large to be human and too rigid to be animal, leave investigators baffled and, honestly, afraid to venture out alone in search of anything else. Something exists in the woods; they are sure of that. They just don't know what it is. The bodies of Mary and Robert "Bob" Robinson are never discovered. Over the next two years, the acres of land is believed to be unsafe for hunting and hiking as multiple animals and hikers turn up missing. Teenagers who venture off in the middle of the night for a fun time see their friends being dragged off into the dark woods by a mysterious creature, "as tall as the trees." Tales of the haunted Robinson Forest in Texas ping social media accounts across the nation, leaving rangers bewildered by multiple unsolved cases. Grace requests that the state fence off the land where only she, as the owner, has access through a gate. The state obliges without hesitation. Reports on missing people decrease. Over the years, the popularity of the forbidden forest dies down, as no one dares to go inside for fear of never coming out. Grace lives alone in the cabin until she passes away at the age of eighty-eight. She had been loved and protected for the rest of her life... and she was happy. The silver coin is never seen again.

The creatures of the forest remain a myth.

THE END

# Acknowledgements

Thank you to my editor, Amy M. Le and her staff at Quill Hawk Publishing for being so very diligent and perceptive. Thank you for teaching me and helping me achieve the best work possible.

I would like to thank my friends and family for your indispensable feedback and patience. I am grateful to those who have been so eager to read my first little novella, and for those who are ready for my next write. Thank you for your love and support.

# About the Author

Kat Hosier is the author of *The Hollow*, her debut novella. Living in Central Oklahoma, she works as a nurse and enjoys cooking, burning in the fire pit, and spending her time at home with her husband and two children. The family owns four pythons, two tarantulas, and a sphynx named Paige. Her traumatic upbringing by her mother sparked several ideas within *The Hollow*. A dream day of hers would consist of preparing a home-cooked meal at the home of Tabitha and Stephen King, while conversing over King's works and life in general.